PUFFIN BOOKS

Pongwiffy and the Goblins' Revenge

Kaye Umansky was born in Plymouth, Devon. Her favourite books as a child were the *Just William* books, *Alice's Adventures in Wonderland*, *The Hobbit* and *The Swish of the Curtain*. She went to teachers' training college, and then she taught in London primary schools for twelve years, specializing in music and drama. In her spare time she sang and played keyboards with a semi-professional soul band.

She now writes full time – or as full time as she can in between trips to Sainsbury's and looking after her husband (Mo), daughter (Ella) and cats (Charlie and Alfie).

PONGWIFFY and the Goblins' Revenge

KAYE UMANSKY

ILLUSTRATED BY CHRIS SMEDLEY

PUFFIN BOOKS

PUFFIN BOOKS

Published by the Penguin Group
Penguin Books Ltd, 80 Strand, London WC2R 0RL, England
Penguin Putnam Inc., 375 Hudson Street, New York, New York 10014, USA
Penguin Books Australia Ltd, 250 Camberwell Road, Camberwell, Victoria 3124, Australia
Penguin Books Canada Ltd, 10 Alcorn Avenue, Toronto, Ontario, Canada M4V 3B2
Penguin Books India (P) Ltd, 11 Community Centre, Panchsheel Park, New Delhi – 110 017, India
Penguin Books (NZ) Ltd, Cnr Rosedale and Airborne Roads, Albany, Auckland, New Zealand
Penguin Books (South Africa) (Pty) Ltd, 24 Sturdee Avenue, Rosebank 2196, South Africa

Penguin Books Ltd, Registered Offices: 80 Strand, London WC2R 0RL, England

www.penguin.com

First published under the title *Broomnapped* by A & C Black (Publishers) Ltd 1991
Published in Puffin Books 1992
14

Text copyright © Kaye Umansky, 1991
Illustrations copyright © Chris Smedley, 1991
All rights reserved

The moral right of the author has been asserted

Set in Monophoto Apollo

Printed in England by Clays Ltd, St Ives plc

Contents

The Cast

Also Starring: The Goblins
Featuring: Woody the Broom
Guest Appearance: Ali Pali the Genie

And:
The Other Brooms
The Rusty Rake
The Coal Shovel
Raiders of the Dump:
Troll with Trolley
Thing with Moonmad 'T' Shirt
Xotindis & Xstufitu, the Mummies
Visiting Zombie from another wood
Arthur the piano playing Dragon

The Entertainers:

Spoon Player with bolt through neck
Barrel organist with paper bag over head (?)
Fortune telling Banshee
Make up/Hair by: Sharkadder
Catering: The Yeti Bros
Pierre de Gingerbeard
Bendyshanks & Sludgegooey (Sandwiches)

Music by: Agglebag & Bagaggle, Macabre & the Witchway Rhythm Boys
Produced by:
Kaye (Today the Book, Tomorrow the Film) Umansky
Graphics: Chris Smedley

CHAPTER ONE

AN EARLY MORNING CRAWLER

Witch Sharkadder was sitting at her dressing table Getting Ready, and it was a serious business. It involved a great deal of preening and pouting in fly-flecked mirrors. It involved the smearing on of various horrid substances which were stored in dozens of mysterious little pots and bottles. Getting Ready needed time, concentration, and above all, quiet. Even Dead Eye Dudley, Sharkadder's cat, knew better than to interrupt when Mistress was Getting Ready.

Sharkadder had been at it for some time now, and had completed the basic groundwork. All facial cracks were filled in, and every inch of her long nose was thoroughly powdered. Her eyelids were painted an evil shade of green and sprouted an alarming pair of spiderleg eyelashes. There were wild splodges of rouge on both cheeks.

Now for the best bit. The final touch. The Lipstick. Sharkadder poured over the delicious possibilities. What should it be today? Hint of Gore? Boiled Beetroot? Squashed Plum Purple? Finally she selected her favourite, Toad Green. Pursing her lips, she leaned forward and carefully ... oh, so carefully ... began to apply it. Then ...

"Yoo hoo! Shaaaaaaaarky! It's me, Pongwiffy. Can I come in?"

This cheery shout was accompanied by wild battering at the door.

Sharkadder jumped like a scalded cat and smeared a greasy trail of Toad Green from chin to earlobe. As the familiar smell wafted in, Dead Eye Dudley peered over the edge of his basket and opened his one good eye.

"Don't let her," advised Dudley. "You'll be sorry."

It was too late. The door crashed open and Witch Pongwiffy stood on the threshold.

"Fancy Dress!" she announced.

"Fancy what?" said Sharkadder.

"That's my latest idea for the Hallowe'en party," explained Pongwiffy, scuttling in and slamming the door behind her. "A Fancy Dress parade. I just had to tell you about it. I say, Sharky, there's this horrible trail of green slime on your face, did you know?

I think something's just died on it. Look, I've brought you a peace offering. A lovely bunch of flowers. I'll just put them in a jug or something.''

Beaming, she produced three drooping dandelions from behind her back, thrust them under Sharkadder's pointed nose, then pushed past and started crashing about in cupboards, looking for a jug or something.

"You've got a cheek," hissed Sharkadder, inspecting the damage in a mirror. "Coming round here, after everything. You've got a nerve."

"Isn't it a lovely morning?" continued Pongwiffy, pretending she hadn't heard. "I woke up and said to Hugo, Hugo, I said, this is just the sort of morning to go and visit my best friend."

"Go visit her, then," suggested Sharkadder coldly.

"Don't be silly. I meant you, of course," explained Pongwiffy.

"Me?" said Sharkadder indignantly. "Your best friend? After what you called me the other night? Ha! Don't make me laugh."

Huffily, she reached for a dirty rag and scrubbed away at the green smear.

"Did I call you something the other night?" asked Pongwiffy, sounding surprised.

"You know you did. An Over-painted Bone Bag With A Face Like A Dead Haddock. I think that was the term."

"Oh, that! You didn't take any notice of *that*, did

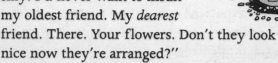

you?" pooh-pooed Pongwiffy, ramming the dandelions any oldhow into an ancient baked bean tin. "I didn't mean it, silly. I'd never want to insult my oldest friend. My *dearest* friend. There. Your flowers. Don't they look nice now they're arranged?"

"No," Sharkadder said frostily. "They don't. I wasn't born yesterday, Pongwiffy. You want something, don't you?"

"Certainly not. I just want to make up, that's all. Look, I apologise. Sorry sorry sorry. There. Now, I'll just pop the kettle on, and we'll have a nice cup of bogwater and a chat, eh? I've missed you, you know, Sharky. I always do when we're not speaking."

Sharkadder sniffed and tossed her hair sullenly. But she was beginning to come round. You could tell.

"I can't wait to tell you all my news," said Pongwiffy, rattling the cups around. "I've been terribly busy working on a brilliant new spell. Guess what? The rubbish is safe! I've finally solved my security problems. Want to know how?"

"Not really," said Sharkadder. She didn't share her friend's enthusiasm for smelly old rubbish. But then, she wasn't Official Dumpkeeper. Pongwiffy was, and she really loved her work. The Dump was her pride and joy. Her hovel, Number 1, Dump Edge, stood right on the edge of it.

"I'll tell you anyway," said Pongwiffy. "I've

invented this amazing magical Wall Of Smell. It's an invisible wall that goes all the way round The Dump. It's so disgusting that nobody can get anywhere near it without a special magic formula which only I know. So ya boo sucks to the raiding parties! They won't get as much as a chair leg this year, I promise you. The famous Witches' Hallowe'en Bonfire will reach even dizzier heights! Aren't I a rotten old spoil-sport?''

"You certainly are," agreed Sharkadder.

"When The Dump's in danger, I'll stick at nothing," announced Pongwiffy. "I'm not sharing my rubbish with any old Troll, Spook or Houri. That's Witch rubbish, that is, and it's going on the Witch bonfire, or my name's not Pongwiffy."

Pongwiffy was rightfully proud of her dump. It had a fine reputation. It had been voted Top of the Tips for three years running. As dumps go, it was the best for miles around. That, of course, made it a prime target for raids. Every year, on the run up to Hallowe'en, it was regularly attacked by all sorts of unsavoury types, looking for choice items to sling on their Hallowe'en bonfires.

At Hallowe'en, there are a lot of parties going on, and a great big bonfire is a MUST. The fact remains, however, that the Witches' Hallowe'en blaze is far and away the best. It's the envy of all, and Pongwiffy likes to keep it that way by all the foul means at her disposal. On the run up to Hallowe'en, therefore, Dump Security becomes A1 Priority. It suddenly bristles with NO TERSPASSERS and PIRVIT KIP-POWT signs. It is patrolled regularly by both Pongwiffy herself and a small, fierce Hamster who goes for the ankles. That's fair enough so far.

But using Magic?

That was cheating.

"It's cheating," said Sharkadder. "The Skeletons won't like it. Neither will the Ghouls. I can't see the Werewolves taking it lying down. There'll be trouble, mark my words."

"Nothing I can't handle," said Pongwiffy confidently. "Hey, I can't wait for tonight's meeting, can you? We're discussing the party, remember? And, Sharky! *Guess whose turn it is to organise it this year*? Mine! And you know what a great organiser I am. I tell you, Sharky, this party will pass into legend. Pong's Great Hallowe'en Party! No, correction. Pongwiffy and *Sharkadder's* Great Hallowe'en Party. Because I want you to help me. You will, won't you? Oh, say you will!"

Sharkadder was tempted. Despite herself, she had missed Pongwiffy. Dead Eye Dudley gave a loud warning cough.

"Listen," continued Pongwiffy. "I found this wonderful book in the rubbish tip. It's called *How To Make Your Party Swing*. That's where I got the fancy dress idea. Sharky, I'm going to make this party swing so high it'll overbalance altogether. I mean, let's face it, the rest of the coven wouldn't know a swinging party if it swung back and bashed 'em in the chops. They need up-to-date sort of Witches like you and me. I'm going to put forward my revolutionary suggestions at the meeting tonight. I bet everyone's dead impressed. No one's ever thought of fancy dress before. Probably haven't even *heard* of it, ha, ha. . ."

Prattling away, Pongwiffy made a confident beeline for the cupboard and got out Sharkadder's biscuit tin, which was clearly marked "Private". She poked around and ate the last chocolate one. She went to Sharkadder's special cake tin and cut herself a huge slice of the fungus sponge which Sharkadder was saving for tea. She found Sharkadder's secret hoard of gingerbread frogs and helped herself to nine. Dudley stationed himself before his tins of Sharkomeat and prepared to fight to the death.

"Make yourself at home," said Sharkadder, heavily sarcastic. She should have thrown Pongwiffy out then and there, of course, but her curiosity was aroused.

"Thanks, I will," said Pongwiffy. She bustled over to the table with a piled plate and two cups of hot, strong bogwater. She stuffed three gingerbread frogs into her mouth, added five sugars to her own cup, and stirred it with the nearest thing to hand, which happened to be Dudley's flea comb. She slumped into a chair, took a huge slurp, wiped her mouth with the sleeve of her old cardigan, placed her boots on the table and sighed with pleasure. Her table manners really were disgraceful. Sharkadder chose to ignore them.

"What's Fancy Dress, then?" asked Sharkadder despite herself.

"Oh, didn't you know? I thought everyone did. Well, it's where you dress up as something and parade around. And the best costume wins first prize. A hamper, I thought, from Swallow and Riskit. You just can't beat their cold skunk pie."

"What — you mean — not wear rags?" said Sharkadder slowly. This really was a novel idea. "Not the hat, or the cloak, or anything?"

"Nope. *Costumes*," explained Pongwiffy, spraying sponge everywhere as she talked. "You know. Pirates. Gypsies. Scarecrows. Cinderella with her Broom. Where's *your* Broom, by the way? I haven't seen it all morning."

"So? It's around," said Sharkadder, suddenly suspicious. It wasn't like Pongwiffy to enquire about an absent Broomstick. "Why?"

"Well, actually, Sharky, I've come to ask you a little favour. I have a slight problem. It's my Broom. It's — er — lost. It's been missing since yesterday. I can't find it anywhere. I was wondering if there's any chance of a lift to Crag Hill tonight. . ."

But she didn't finish.

"I knew it!" howled Sharkadder, enraged. "Hear that, Dudley? I *knew* she wouldn't come crawling round here unless she wanted something!"

"I told you," said Dudley. "I warned you."

"But Sharky! I've simply *got* to be there. We're planning the *Party*," wailed Pongwiffy. "Surely you don't begrudge your best friend a ride on your mangy Broomstick?"

"Yes," said Sharkadder. "I do. And you know how Dudley feels about Hugo. How do you feel about sharing our Broom with Pongwiffy's nasty little Hamster, Duddles, darling? Be honest."

Dudley spat on the floor.

"You see?" said Sharkadder.

"Ah Sharky, please!" wheedled Pongwiffy. "Be reasonable. I can't possibly walk to Crag Hill. It's miles! Besides, if I don't come, I won't be able to see what you're wearing. And you always look so nice on these occasions."

"True," said Sharkadder, tossing her hair. She loved a compliment. "I am rather eye-catching, aren't I?"

"You are, you certainly are. You're the most fashionable Witch in the coven by miles. That's why I want YOU to judge the Fancy Dress parade. Oh, please say you'll take me. Do."

"Wellllll. . ."

"Don't," warned Dudley. "She called you a haddock, remember? Don't."

"Shut *up*, Dudley,"
said Pongwiffy. "This
is a private conversation
between Witches and nothing
to do with you.
What d'you say, Sharky?"

But Sharkadder never got the chance to say anything, because right at that moment the door burst
open with an almighty crash!

CHAPTER TWO

STICK WARP

There, poised on the threshold, was Pongwiffy's missing Broomstick. It was as white as a sheet, which was unusual, because it was normally a healthy mahogany. It swept in and made for the nearest dark corner. Once there it sagged against the wall breathing hard, obviously terribly agitated.

"Badness gracious me," exclaimed Sharkadder. "Whatever next!"

"Aha! So there you are!" snapped Pongwiffy sternly. "I've been looking for you everywhere, you idiot. What d'you think you're up to, barging in here like that? Bad Broom! Go outside again, and come in properly."

The Broom cowered pathetically.

"What's wrong with it?" asked Sharkadder, poking it curiously with a long, bony finger. "Why isn't it obeying you? Brooms are supposed to obey."

"How should I know? It's not usually like this. Stand up straight, Broom, and do as you're told, or it's the axe for you."

There was a clonk, and the Broom promptly passed out on the floor.

"It's fainted," remarked Sharkadder. "It must have been what you said about the axe."

"Funny," said Pongwiffy, dousing the Broom with tepid bogwater. "It can usually take a joke."

The Broom sneezed, spluttered and attempted to rise.

"Get up, you. Chop chop!" ordered Pongwiffy. Which was the worst thing she could have said, because the Broom swooned again.

"Oh, frog warts! It's passed out again. I wonder what's wrong with it? If only it could tell me."

(It's a funny thing about Broomsticks. They can understand English but they can't speak it. That's because they speak only Wood. Wood is a highly specialised language in which the Brooms have dull wooden conversations about the problems of getting into corners and the discomfort of flying head first into a north wind. To us and the Witches it just sounds like a lot of rustling.)

"It's probably just a touch of stick warp," said Sharkadder. She was feeling smug. Her Broom was better quality than Pongwiffy's and never gave trouble. "Why don't you just ask it? Try casting that Language Spell. You know, that one we learnt at school. How's it go? Zithery zithery zoom, I want to speak to my Broom. You know. That one."

"No fear," said Pongwiffy. "I tried it once, out of curiosity. Terrible experience. Take my advice, never try talking Wood. Horrible side effects. Splinters in the mouth. Shocking taste of sawdust.

Besides, the effects last for ages. It's not just limited to Brooms, you know. You can understand anything wooden. Who wants to know what dreary old shed doors and dull floorboards and stodgy old trees are yapping on about for weeks on end? I tell you, I nearly died of boredom. I'd sooner be stuck in a lift with a Goblin."

At the word "Goblin", the Broom suddenly gave a convulsive heave and reared upright. Once vertical, it tottered groggily towards the door. Pongwiffy shot her hand out and grabbed it firmly by the stick.

"Oops!" she said. "Looks like I shouldn't have said that either."

"What? Goblin?"

"Yes. Stop it, Broom! Steady on!"

"Goblin?" repeated Sharkadder, enjoying the effect it had on the Broom. "Did you say Goblin? It doesn't like the word Goblin? That's interesting. *Goblin*, you say?"

"Look, do you have to keep saying that?" complained Pongwiffy, fighting for control as the Broom struggled in her grasp.

"Saying what?" enquired Sharkadder, all innocence.

"Goblin. Oh, bother! Now you've made *me* say it. Stop it, you, before I lose my temper!"

That was to the Broom, who was getting itself into a terrible state, scrabbling and straining to get away.

"This is interesting. There's a clue here," said

Sharkadder. "Let's think for a moment. It doesn't like AXE, CHOP CHOP, and GOBLIN. That suggests to me that it's scared that GOBLINS might come after it with an AXE and CHOP IT UP! Well, I suppose they might as well, really. I mean, look at it. It's useless. Hey, Broom! There's a Goblin right behind you! Ha, ha ha!"

"Shush, you idiot!" yelled Pongwiffy. But it was too late. The Broom finally flipped. It twisted from her grasp and hurtled around the room, smashing into Sharkadder's dressing table and sending a lifetime's collection of rare beauty aids crashing down in an explosion of lurid face powders, greasy lipstick and small bottles of gloppy stuff.

"Ah, no!" screeched Sharkadder. "My make-up! Anything but that!"

"Come back here, you! Heel!" howled Pongwiffy, stamping her foot. "Oh, my badness. It's bolting! Stop it! It's out of control!"

It certainly was. It was like a mad thing, that Broom. Not content with the murder of Sharkadder's

make-up, it knocked over the hat stand, the cauldron and three chairs before skidding in a dish of Sharkomeat and landing on Dudley's tail. Dudley swore and bit it in the stick. Sharkadder looked up from the multi-coloured puddles at her feet, screamed, and attempted to do the same. The Broom dodged to one side, then launched itself at the window, intent on escape.

Pongwiffy, with great presence of mind, stuck out her foot. The Broom, blind with panic, tripped over and crashed heavily to the floor. Pongwiffy leapt on top of it and got it in a firm stranglehold.

"Behave yourself, you idiot!" she screeched.

"Look at the mess you've made. Sweep it up this minute, or I'll chop you into clothes pegs!"

But there was no point in any further discussion. The Broom was out for the count and no amount of bullying could do the trick.

"Now see what you've done!" Pongwiffy wailed to Sharkadder, accusingly. "Look at it! Stiff as a – well, stiff as a Broomstick. I'll never be able to ride it tonight. I'm grounded! Oh, Sharky, you've got to give me a lift to the meeting. Please!"

"No," wept Sharkadder, on her knees beside the ruins of her make-up. "Never, never, never. Not in a million trillion years. Not if you beg on bended knees. Not if you cringe and crave and implore. Not after what your Broom just did."

"Not if I buy you a brand new collection of make-up? As well as let you judge the fancy dress parade?"

Sharkadder hesitated.

"Can I be *in* the fancy dress parade as well as judge it?"

"Certainly," said Pongwiffy immediately. "Nothing could be fairer."

"Done," said Sharkadder briskly. "See you in your garden at midnight."

CHAPTER THREE

{ ? ? ' ' ? ? ' ? ' ? ? ? ? ? ?

A BRUSH WITH DANGER

By now, of course, you'll be dying to know what had happened to Pongwiffy's Broom. Why should a normally level-headed, sensible Broomstick suddenly fly off the handle like that?

Well, it had good reason. The day before, you see, it had had a terrible shock. Something awful had happened to it.

It had been Broomnapped by Goblins!

It had happened so easily. The day before had been Wednesday, and Woody was bored. (That's its name, by the way. Woody. Nobody but other Brooms ever bothers to call it anything but Broom, but as it's starring in this part of the story, you really should know its name.)

So. Woody was bored. Being a Witch of dirty habits, Pongwiffy never gave it anything to do. She liked her hovel just as it was (filthy). Understandably Woody, who was an active type, got tired of being propped up in the garden shed with nothing to do for hours on end except listen to an indescribably tedious game of I Spy between a rusty rake and an old coal shovel.

Lunch was over. Woody had swept the shed floor at least a dozen times, and the long afternoon seemed to stretch into infinity.

"Bored," thought Woody. "That's what I am.

Bored stiff. Fed up to the back bristles. Unamused. I must find something to do, or I'll go stark staring bonkers.''

It sneaked into the hovel and tried a bit of furtive sweeping when Pongwiffy's back was turned, but she noticed.

''Oi! You! I've told you before about that! You leave that dirt right where it is!''

Feeling fed up and generally unappreciated, Woody flounced out and went looking for Hugo, Pongwiffy's Hamster. Hugo couldn't speak Wood either, but was too kind to mind when the lonely Broom moped around after him. However, this particular morning Hugo was nowhere to be found as he was out checking for weak points in Pongwiffy's Wall Of Smell.

Looking for a Hamster (even one wearing a gas mask) in a rubbish tip is like looking for a tick in a Goblin's sum book. You're just wasting your time. Woody poked around a bit, then gave up.

''Now what?'' it thought. It looked up. The sky was a huge, empty sweep of tempting blue, just crying out to be flown in.

"I know," thought Woody. "I'll go for a quiet little fly, all on my own. Brush up my flying techniques. Bit of wind in the bristles, that's the ticket."

Now, this wasn't strictly allowed. The Witch rule book firmly states that Broomsticks MUST NOT fly:

1) During daylight hours.
2) Without a Witch, unless given written permission.

But if you're bored, you get tempted into doing all kinds of silly things. Just this once, Woody decided to risk it. After all, Witchway Wood was at its quietest this hour of the day. Most of the Witches would be sleeping off lunch, and it was unlikely that it would be noticed. Feeling rather wicked, it did a couple of pre-flight exercises, just to get the sap moving - what Brooms call timbering up – then it

took a deep breath, flexed at the base, and gave a little jump. Up it soared, over the tree tops, into a nice, warm southerly wind.

"Mmmmm," thought Woody. "Now, this is more like it. Just what the tree surgeon ordered."

Indeed it felt wonderfully free, up there among the clouds without Pongwiffy's bony knees jabbing into its stick.

"Wow!" thought Woody. "It's good to be alive and a Broom today. And it skittishly performed an easy somersault or two, then attempted a complicated triple stick loop followed by an inverted back flip. As usual it didn't quite manage it. To avoid loss of face, it chased a passing crow for a minute or so, then flipped over on its back and floated lazily on the air currents. It was enjoying itself so much, it didn't really pay any attention to where it was flying.

Where was it flying?

Directly over Goblin Territory, that's where!

Goblin Territory. That's the name given to the scrubby, stony slopes of the Lower Misty Mountains which border the south-western edges of Witchway Wood. It's an unpopular, lonely, desolate place. There are a lot of sharp rocks up there, and it usually drizzles. To be truthful, as a tourist area, it lacks something. Never the less, it is home to seven particularly stupid Goblins, who live in a cave and answer to the names of Plugugly, Stinkwart, Hog, Slopbucket, Lardo, Eyesore and Sproggit. That

makes seven. One whole Gaggle.

Now, Goblins and Witches are sworn enemies, and usually prefer to live at least a thousand miles apart, so you may wonder why this particular Gaggle choose to live right next door to Witchway Wood, which is notoriously stiff with the old girls.

Wonder no more. Plugugly, Stinkwart, Hog, Slopbucket, Lardo, Eyesore and Sproggit didn't choose. They had been dumped there by Magic, and there, much to their disgust, they had to stay.

It hadn't always been that way. In the old days they were regular gypsies, always moving around, looking for fresh neighbours to drive mad. Until that fateful occasion when they were stupid enough to attempt squatting in a Wizard's house. The furious house-holder came back, took one look at the scandalous state of his kitchen, and cast a Spell of Banishment which whisked them away to this particular cave on this particular mountain. Right next door to Witchway Wood.

The Goblins, when they had got over their surprise, were terribly fed up. The cave was damp and there was nothing to eat. The only place to go hunting was down in the woods, where the Witches took great pleasure in spotting them, swatting them and booting them back to their own territory again in two whisks of a wand. Not that the Goblins ever succeeded in catching anything anyway. They were much too stupid. Hungry, harrassed, hounded and frequently rained on, they had a very lean time of it.

Woody was aware of all this. Sadly, though, it was unaware that it was flying directly above Goblin Territory. It only discovered this when it was rudely knocked out of the air by a large brick.

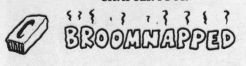

CHAPTER FOUR

The brick had been thrown by young Sproggit. Sproggit hadn't actually been aiming at Woody, although he boasted later that he had. He hadn't even noticed that there was a Broom up there. He'd just thrown a brick because he felt like it. (Throwing bricks is typically Goblinish behaviour.) So Sproggit was extremely surprised when his brick connected with Woody, bringing the poor thing crashing down out of the sky, point first onto his own foot.

Sproggit's pained scream brought the rest of the Gaggle pouring from their cave. When they saw what had happened, they were delirious with joy. A captured Broomstick! What luck! Even better, it was that ol' Pongwiffy's Broomstick. What a prize! What a break!

Poor Woody. They threw it about a bit, jumped on it a couple of times, then tied it up and triumphantly bore it back into the cave. Thankfully, Woody was stunned, and didn't know about any of this. Crash landing on your sharp end from a great height is no joke.

When it came round some time later, it was horrified to find itself gagged, bound, chained and firmly padlocked to a rusty hook projecting from the wall of a dank, smelly cave. A short distance away, torches flickered on the boots, braces and bobble hats of its seven unsavoury captors, who were huddled in a conspiratorial circle, obviously plotting.

"Oh no!" groaned Woody to itself. "Captured by Goblins! How embarrassing. Think of the shame. If the gang get to hear about this, I'll be the laughing stick of the sky. And I'm not even supposed to *be* here. Supposing Mistress finds out? I'll never live it down ..."

Anxiously, it looked around for a means of escape. There wasn't one. The ropes were so tight, its sap was cut off. Even if it could somehow wriggle free, the front boulder was firmly shut.

"How depressing," thought Woody. "Alone and friendless in a cave of mad Goblins. What will become of me?"

Sick to the stick, it slumped back hopelessly and reluctantly tuned in to the Goblin's conversation.

"Let's chop it up." That was young Sproggit. "I cort it, din I? An' I say we chops it up. Wiv an axe. Chop it up an' send it back to ol' Pongwiffy in liddle pieces. Chop chop."

Whaaattttt?????!! Woody's sap ran cold.

"Sproggit's right," agreed Slopbucket. "She's gorrit comin' to 'er she 'as, that ol' Pongwiffy. Bein' so mean wiv 'er rubbish. Stickin' up that there Waller Smell, the ol' cheat."

That brought a heartfelt chorus of agreement. Feelings were running high about Pongwiffy's Wall Of Smell. Raiding the Dump on the run up to Hallowe'en was traditional. Everyone did it. Using Magic to guard it was downright mean.

"Booo!"

"Unfair!"

" 'Ere 'ere!"

"Down wiv de Waller Smell."

"That's settled then," nodded Sproggit. "Chop it up. Chop chop. Thas the ticket."

" 'Ang about," interrupted the biggest Goblin, nearly bursting with eagerness. His name was Plug-ugly, and *he had an idea!* This was a novel experience for him. "Nar, look, listen! I gorran idear. A ransom note. See, 'ere's wot we do. We writes dis note to ol'

Pongwiffy sayin' as 'ow we got 'er Broom 'ostage an' we demands a bagger gold. 'Ow's dat?''

Of the two plans, Woody much preferred Plugugly's. However, to its dismay, it found itself in a minority. Everyone thought Plugugly's suggestion was terrible and said so. A ransom note? Hah! Gold? Poo! What was the point of gold? There was nowhere to spend it, stranded as they were in the wilds of the Lower Misty Mountains. But Plugugly didn't want to abandon his idea.

"Orl right! Orl right den," he shouted above the boos. "Ferget de gold. Let's arsk fer sumpfin else. Der...... I gorrit! A free bagger rubbish, fer our Hallowe'en bonfire. Better still, an invite to der Witches' Hallowe'en Party!"

This idea was greeted by mocking howls of derision. Go to an old Witch party? Not on your nelly! Why, no Goblin worth his braces would be seen dead at an old Witch party. What was Plugugly thinking of? Where was his pride? Etc etc.

"But dey always 'as a better time den we do," argued Plugugly stubbornly. "Dey always got balloons. An' funny 'ats. An' stuff to eat. An' dere's dancin'. An' dat gurt big bonfire. Put ours to shame last year, dat gurt big bonfire. I mean, even wivout de Waller Smell, we never seems to make a successful raid, do we? We always gets foiled."

The Goblins nodded and gnashed their teeth, green with envy. It was true. These Witches knew both how to protect their rubbish and how to celebrate in style. Every year, on Hallowe'en night, the Goblins had a miserable time sharing a small pot of boiled stinging nettles around a titchy, sad, damp apology for a bonfire, whilst over on Crag Hill, the Witches merrily pigged themselves on sausages and baked spuds by the light of a crackling conflagration that lit the sky for miles around. And why? Because that mean ol' Pongwiffy always got the pick of the rubbish and refused to share, that's why.

"Well, anyway, a ransom note's out," remarked Stinkwart, who had suddenly thought of something.

"Why?"

"Cos none of us can write," explained Stinkwart.   And that was true too.

"I still say we chop it up," insisted Sproggit stubbornly. "No one's 'ad a better idear. I mean, what else kin yer do wiv a Witch's Broomstick?"

There followed a long silence, while the Goblins thought about what you could do with a Witch's Broomstick. It wasn't often they had a stroke of luck like this. They must be able to turn it to their advantage.

Over in the shadows, the subject under discussion swallowed hard and trembled.

" 'Ere! We kin burn it," volunteered Lardo in a flash of inspiration. "We kin make a bonfire of it, see, an' set light to it. 'Ere! We kin do it on 'allowe'en!

As a sorter protest, see. That'd really spite them Witches.''

"Hooray!" cheered Slopbucket. "Let's do that!"

" 'T woulden make much of a blaze," pointed out Eyesore. "Look 'ow thin it is. Only last a minute or two.''

Woody shuddered at the thought. It really didn't like the way the conversation was going.

"Chop it up. Chop it up," intoned young Sproggit, eyes glazed.

"Shame there's just the one," said Hog. "If we 'ad more'n one, there'd be a decent blaze. But we don't.''

"Chop it up. Chop it up.''

"Wait a tick," said Plugugly suddenly. " 'Ang about. I fink – it's comin', don't rush me – I fink I gorra plan!''

The Goblins didn't look convinced.

"No, really," insisted Plugugly. "I 'ave. Listen. All right, so one Broomstick don't make a bonfire, I kin see dat. But like 'Og says, a lot of 'em would! So why stick at de one? Let's capture anuvver one, and 'ave .. er.......... free. Or is it four? Anyway, you get de idear. Den we'll capture anuvver one and anuvver one. See? Den, when we got all of 'em, we hides 'em so de Witches don't know where dey is.''

"Where?" asked Eyesore.

"I dunno yet, I ain't worked out all de details. Down a 'ole or sumpfin. But you get the gen'ral idear? We takes 'em 'ostage, den we tell de Witches we'll set fire to 'em, unless dey agrees to our demands. An' if we can't fink of any demands, we'll burn 'em anyway."

There was a pause, while the Goblins thought about it.

"See?" said Plugugly proudly. "Told yer I 'ad a plan, din I?"

"Issa plan all right," agreed Eyesore. "But it's full of 'oles, innit? I mean, 'ow we gonner get our 'ands on the rest of the Brooms? Eh? I mean, they aint gonner conveniently fly this way so young Sproggit 'ere kin knock 'em outer the sky wiv bricks, are they? They're not all dozey like this one."

Beneath its ropes, Woody nearly died of shame.

"Eyesore's right," agreed Slopbucket. "The Witches keep 'em locked up at night. We'll never get away wiv it."

"Chop it up. Chop it up," droned young Sproggit.

"Wait a minute," insisted Plugugly. Success had gone to his head, and the ideas seemed to be positively bursting out. "Dere's one time when we could do it. Tomorrer night. Coven night. We could do it while de Witches are 'avin' dere meetin' up on Crag 'Ill. All de Brooms are in de Broom Park, right? All conveenently in de one place, see? Now what we does is, we sneaks up, under covera darkness, like, den we. . . . .''

" ' 'Arf a tick! I 'eard a noise. That there Broom's awake and snooping on our plans!'' broke in Lardo. "Come on, boys! Let's tease it. Tease break!''

Everyone welcomed the diversion. All this plotting and planning was all very well, but it made the brains tired. A tease break was just what was needed.

Poor Woody. Suddenly surrounded, it tried to look proud and indifferent as the Goblins poked fun.

"Chop chop,'' taunted Sproggit, pretending he had an axe. "Chop chop.''

"Where's the matches? Somebody fetch me the matches!'' bawled Lardo. Eyesore did a mocking monkey dance, and everyone fell about laughing.

"You know, I never seen a Witch Broomstick this close to before,'' said Hog, wiping his eyes. "Nuffin' special, is it? Wonder 'ow it works?''

"Dunno,'' said Slopbucket. "I s'pose there's a

Magic Word or sumpfin."

"Sure to be," agreed Lardo. " 'Ere! Wouldn't it be good if we knew wot it was? Then we could 'ave a go at flyin' it. Worra larf eh?"

The Goblins looked at each other, amazed that they hadn't thought of that before. Fly it! Of course! They slapped their knees at the thought of the laugh it would be.

" 'Ere!" continued Lardo. "Let's just try it wiv a few words, eh? Never know, we might hit on the right one."

The Goblins thought about possible words.

"Aber Cadaber." (That was Eyesore.)

"Open Sesame Seed?" (Hog, not too confidently.)

"Eeny Meeny Miny Mo!" (Stinkwart)

"Fee fi fo fum. . . ." (Slopbucket)

" 'Ubble bubble toil and whatsit. . ."

" 'Ickery Dickory Dock. . . . ."

Through it all, to its credit, Woody managed to maintain an aloof air of distain. The suggestions got more and more stupid, and finally trailed out altogether.

" 'S no good," remarked Eyesore. "It ain't gonner fly, an' that's that. Tell you what, though. Seein' as it's our slave, an' it's anuvver week before we burns it, it might as well do a bit o' sweepin'. Place could do wiv it."

"Good idear," said Hog. "Cut it loose, Sproggit. Plugugly, roll back that boulder a bit. We'll get a bit o' fresh air in 'ere. All this plottin's makin' my throat sore."

Woody could hardly believe its luck. It held its breath as Sproggit fumbled with ropes and chains and padlocks, armed only with his teeth and an old fork. At the same time, Plugugly waddled over to the front boulder, and moved it an inch or two to one side. Freedom was in sight.

"Right, orf yer go," commanded Lardo. "Let's see yer do yer stuff. Sweep!"

Woody didn't need to be told twice. It swept all right. It swept Sproggit to one side and Lardo to the other. It swept a clean path through the rest of the Goblins, cleverly avoided Plugugly, who was too big to be swept, squeezed through the gap in the boulder, flung itself into the air and was off like a bat out of hell before the Goblins knew what had hit them.

Whooosh. Gone. Just like that.

Dawn was breaking as Woody flew homeward. That meant it had been in the Goblin cave all night! Oh dear. What a disaster.

As it flew, Woody's mind was a jumbled mass of seething emotions. Sheer, blessed relief, of course. That was top of the list. But after that, shame. Caught by Goblins, of all things. Why, everyone knew the Goblins never caught anything. Even a glow worm could outwit a Goblin, because Goblins were *stupid*. Oh, idiot, idiot!

It sunk further into gloom as it reflected on what would happen if the story got out. A public warning at the very least. Most probably be grounded for weeks. The other Brooms would be ashamed of it. People would point, and say in loud, sneery voices, "There goes the Broom that got captured by Goblins". Worst of all, it would have to face Pongwiffy, who would go on and on and on and on and *on*. She might even do what she was always threatening, and chop it up for clothes pegs. Oh horror.

But wait. There was a glimmer of hope. As far as it knew, there had been no witnesses. If the Goblins kept their mouths shut, there was a good chance that no one would ever know. Pongwiffy probably hadn't even missed it. Woody cheered up. Perhaps things weren't so bad after all.

But wait again. *What about the Goblins' plan?* Supposing they went through with it? Supposing they did indeed come creeping up on the defenceless Broomsticks when they were all alone in the Broom Park? Just think of it. A mass broomnapping, and all because Woody had failed to give a warning. What would happen to its friends? More important, what would happen to IT??!!

Woody wasn't keen to find out. Best not go to Crag Hill tomorrow night. Just as a safety precaution. Though, of course, nothing was really going to happen, was it? The Goblins would never do it, would they? They hadn't got the brains to organise something like that, had they? So there wasn't any point in mentioning it, really, was there? No, of course not.

Woody was no hero. It had made its mind up. It would keep its mouth shut, go sick and hope for the best. Which is why we find it being dragged by a very fed-up Pongwiffy back down Sharkadder's path. Insensible and in disgrace. The cause of yet another major bust-up.

Ouch!

CHAPTER FIVE

"Come on, you lump of dead wood," Pongwiffy growled through gritted teeth as she stomped through the woods. "Just you wait 'til I get you home."

She was in a terrible mood. The sound of Shark-adder's slammed door was still ringing in her ears, and she felt quite queasy from eating all that humble pie. The last thing she felt like doing was dragging the comatose Broom all the way home to Number 1, Dump Edge.

Autumn leaves lay thickly on the ground, disguising various hazards, some of which were painful and some squelchy. Deep holes, sharp stones, stinging nettles, rabbit droppings – you name it, Pongwiffy fell down it, tripped over it, brushed against it or stepped in it. The Broom was not so much heavy as awkward. It got tangled in scratchy bushes and wedged in tree roots. It trailed through boggy puddles. It was a liability.

Squelch! More droppings. Haggis ones, most likely.

"Oh, badness!" Pongwiffy screeched to the Broom, at the end of her tether. "I've had enough of this! I'm going to leave you here to rot, that's what I'm going to do!"

And she just might have done it too. But, just at that moment, there was an interesting turn of events. It happened with no warning. There was a sudden large puff of sickly green smoke, a spray of luminous green sparks, and... *a Genie appeared!*

Isn't that astounding?

As well as the smoke and the sparks, the Genie was accompanied by quite a loud thunderclap, causing several birds to fall out of trees and a passing rabbit to be treated for shock. Even Pongwiffy, who, being a Witch, was used to these things, was mildly surprised. You didn't often get Genies in Witchway Wood. It just wasn't their sort of place. Rotten climate. Terrible food. Hardly any shops. No decent bazaars or coffee houses. No dancing girls or fire-eaters. And all those terrible old Witches.

"Bother, bother, bother!" sighed the Genie, staring around, obviously unimpressed. "Not another wood. I have taken yet another wrong turning. How incredibly ghastly."

"Watch it, Tubby," snapped Pongwiffy. "This isn't just another wood. This is Witchway Wood. I live here. So mind your tongue."

This particular Genie did, in fact, have a weight problem which his traditional skimpy Genie attire did little to hide. He wore a filmy blouse thing with big, puffy sleeves under a red fringed bolero. The blouse thing was quite short, and there was a fair amount of *tummy* sticking out between that and the wide scarlet sash which held up his pants. The pants were made from some flimsy material which tended to cling. On his head was a red turban. He wore far, far too much jewellery. He twinkled and clinked with trinkets, rings and bangles. Medallions swung from him like baubles on a Christmas tree. At his feet (which boasted ostentatious, curly-toed slippers), lay a shabby old carpet bag. He looked very out of place.

His name was Ali Pali, and indeed he *was* out of place. He was also out of luck. Beneath all the flashy gear, Ali was a very worried Genie. The reason he was worried was because he was lampless. He had lost his lamp and had nowhere to go. Being without a lamp made him very vulnerable. (That's why he had a weight problem. Being vulnerable made him eat a lot.)

The reason he had no lamp to return to was simple. Somebody had dropped it. Luckily Ali was out at the time: answering a rub, building a magical palace or something. While he was gone, some nosey idiot had picked the lamp up to look at it, fumbled, then dropped it on the floor, where it smashed into a thousand pieces. Poor Ali. He came back to find that he had lost everything, including all his nice clothes and his carefully hoarded treasure (which had been hidden up the spout).

Every Genie lives in dread of this happening. To be without a lamp is to be mocked and sneered at by other Genies. It means you don't get invited to dinner any more. It means you have to take a *proper* job! Horrors!

Ali had to find another lamp immediately. He had to get another lid over his head without delay. The trouble was, lamps were expensive. Somehow, he would have to get enough gold together for a down payment. But how?

What was needed was some sort of gigantic fiddle. Something which would earn him an instant fortune. Ali was rather hoping that something of this sort would present itself. On the surface, Witchway Wood didn't appear all that promising - although, funnily enough, hadn't he noticed something about it the other day in the *Genie Journal*? A small, tucked-away article about a Wall Of Smell which some nutty old Witch had constructed in order to keep the local riffraff from raiding her rubbish dump. Now, what was her name again?

Waving away the last of the green smoke, Ali Pali found himself face to face with the woman who had just spoken. Politely, he bared his teeth in his most charming smile and did one of those bows that should ideally be accompanied by the clash of cymbals.

"A thousand pardons, madam," he said smoothly. "No offence intended, I am sure. Allow me to introduce myself. My name is Ali Pali. I am a Genie by profession. Ali Pali is my name, granting wishes is my game, ha ha. I am delighted to meet you. I trust you were not startled by my sudden appearance. Please. Allow me to offer you a little present. It is customary amongst us Genies to do this when we meet new friends."

Still smiling his oily smile, Ali gave a theatrical snap of the fingers. There was a little puff of pink smoke, looking for all the world like airborne candyfloss, and he cleverly produced a gift-wrapped boxfull of pink turkish delight, which floated temptingly through the air, slowly opening its own lid as it came towards Pongwiffy.

"Get it off me!" snarled Pongwiffy, swiping bad-temperedly at the box. " I hate turkish delight. You Genies make me sick. You're all the same. To you it might be just another wood, but to us Witches, it's home. Clear off. You can't bribe me with your silly, sickly, pink, little spells. Nobody asked you to come."

Traditionally, Witches don't trust Genies. They look down their noses at that sort of flash in the pan, showy oriental magic. They hate their towny ways and the clothes. Witches consider that Genies are too flash by half.

"You are right. Please. I meant no rudeness to your wood," said Ali Pali quickly, snapping his fingers. The rejected turkish delight floated back to him, then down into the carpet bag, which opened all by itself to receive it.

"I'm just not dressed for it, you see. I am sure if I lived here I would love it. Nature. The great outdoors. The crisp smell of an Autumn morning . . ."

Enthusiastically, he threw his arms wide, took a step forward and tripped over Woody. He stumbled, waving his arms wildly. One golden slipper sank into a pile of something unpleasant.

"Watch out, clumsy. That's my Broom you're treading on," scolded Pongwiffy.

Ali Pali scraped his foot off on a clump of grass. One of his medallions had got tangled up in a nearby bramble bush, but he still managed to keep smiling. He was a real pro.

"A thousand sorries. I sincerely apologise. But tell me. Your Broom. Why is it like this? Is it sick?"

"What's it look like?" snapped Pongwiffy.

"Hmm." Ali Pali nudged Woody with a curly toe. "Can I help in any way? I have a few tricks up my sleeve. I have a certain way with flying carpets. If you would allow me to examine it, perhaps I . . ."

"Look, do you mind?" said Pongwiffy, bristling crossly. This Genie was really beginning to get on her nerves. "You're talking to a Witch, remember? I could fix it myself if I wanted to. It so happens that I don't want to, that's all."

"Oh, fool, fool that I am!" wailed Ali Pali, striking his head, in an agony of remorse. "Of course you can fix it yourself! Why am I offering a Witch my help, poor pathetic conjuror that I am? Forgive me. If Witch Magic can't fix it, nothing can. I know that. Powerful stuff, Witch Magic. All those brews you do. All that mysterious chanting and cackling, eh? Amazing results. That Wall Of Smell, for instance. Everyone is talking about it. Even the Wizards are impressed. There's a whole article about it in the *Genie Journal*. Most interesting. Now, what was the name of the Witch who created it. . . it's on the tip of my tongue. . .?"

Pongwiffy couldn't believe her ears. This was too good to be true.

"Me! Pongwiffy! It's me!" she burst out, unable to contain herself. "I did it! It's my Wall. What paper was it in, did you say?"

To Pongwiffy's amazement, Ali Pali suddenly did something very unexpected. He took her hand and planted a wet, unpleasant kiss on it!

"Get off," snapped Pongwiffy, snatching her hand back and wiping it on her sleeve. "Yuck."

"A thousand rejoicings!" crowed Ali Pali, hopping from one curly slipper to the other, jangling his bracelets, beside himself with pleasure. "Luck is with me this day! That's the name! Witch Pongwiffy! *The* Witch Pongwiffy. What an honour. Just wait till I tell the rest of the guys."

"Well," said Pongwiffy, terribly pleased and flattered. "Well, fancy that. Me in the paper."

"I am so excited!" babbled Ali Pali, wild with enthusiasm. "The creator of the famous Wall Of Smell herself! I am your number one fan. If only I could do such Magic!"

"Oh, you probably could, in time," said Pongwiffy graciously. She found herself warming towards this unusually charming and intelligent Genie. "Walls Of Smell are a doddle, as a matter of fact. Kid's stuff. You only need the basic brew."

"Please. Do not mock me. Ali Pali knows his limitations. I am but an apprentice at the craft. Pretty fireworks. Coloured lights. Pigeons. Special effects. Transformations. That's about my level. But make a *brew*? Alas. I would not know where to start. But, please. Make a humble Genie happy. I'd take it as a great honour if you'd allow me to help you carry your sick stick home."

He bowed deeply, smiled toothily, and held out a packet of sherbet lemons.

"Sweetie?" he said.

Now, normally, Pongwiffy would have seen through all this. Warning bells would have rung, and she would have seen through his little game no trouble. But the events of the morning had frazzled her brains. She wasn't thinking straight. Right now, she just wanted to get home. The Genie had such a nice manner. And she was particularly partial to sherbet lemons. . .

"All right," she said graciously. "You take the bristle end."

And together they set off.

"I wouldn't normally be doing this," remarked Pongwiffy. "We're not supposed to fraternize with you lot."

"Quite right, best to be wary," agreed Ali Pali. "You can't trust anybody these days. What a charming wood this is. One moment, please. My flimsy pants are hooked up on this delightful bramble bush."

Pongwiffy waited while he sorted himself out. There was a nasty tearing sound. They walked on in silence for a bit. Then:

"I suppose you are not allowed to talk about your great power," said Ali Pali. "Such a pity. You have such an interesting personality. I could write an in-depth article for the Journal about you. *Pongwiffy -the Witch Beneath The Smell*. That sort of thing."

"Oh, I don't mind talking about myself," said Pongwiffy graciously. "As long as you keep it general. But don't expect me to give away any trade secrets, ha ha! Any more of those sherbet lemons?''

''Certainly, certainly, here, take the packet,'' said Ali Pali. ''So you don't mind if I ask you a couple of questions, then?''

''Fire away,'' said Pongwiffy amiably.

''The Wall Of Smell. What's it made of?'' asked Ali Pali, trying not to sound too eager.

''Aha,'' said Pongwiffy. ''Old family recipe.''

''Oh, go on!'' coaxed Ali Pali. ''You can trust me. As one professional to another, eh? I thought I detected just a hint – a mere hint, mind – of garlic. Am I right?''

''Certainly,'' agreed Pongwiffy, caught off guard. ''Anti-vampire, garlic. Everyone knows that.''

''Phew!'' whistled Ali Pali, lost in admiration. ''Garlic. Brilliant!''

''The rest is just the usual,'' went on Pongwiffy. ''All standard stuff. Eight ounces of Eau de Stable. Four drops of Hint of Pigsty. A tablespoonful of Olde Socke. Two bad eggs. Stagnant Pond to mix. Oh, and a pinch of Essence of Ashtray. You mix it all up and leave to fester and ferment overnight. Then you sling it in the cauldron at Mark 6. . .''

And so on. Ali nodded admiringly, filing it all away in his brain for future use.

''Incredible!'' he said, when Pongwiffy finally stopped talking. ''Of course, your Wall Of Smell is not exactly popular, is it? I don't agree, of course, but some say you Witches are mean old cheats. They say it wouldn't hurt to share the rubbish out a bit.

Hallowe'en goodwill and so on. What do you say to that?''

Pongwiffy shrugged.

"Witches *are* mean old cheats,'' she pointed out. "That's what being a Witch is all about. If we wanted to be fair and generous we'd join the Brownies. You can quote me on that. You know what, Ali, I'm really enjoying talking to you. Any more questions?''

Such pleasant conversation helped pass the time, and finally they reached smelling distance of the Dump.

"Nearly there,'' said Pongwiffy happily. "Do you want to come in for a cup of bogwater or something? Then you can have a closer sniff of the Wall Of Smell.''

"Er – no, sadly I have an appointment,'' said Ali Pali, hastily dropping his end of Woody and fumbling up his sleeve for a handkerchief. "I think we must part here. But may I say what a pleasure it's been talking to you. I do hope we meet again.''

And, with a charming little wave, he vanished.

"What a delightful Genie,'' thought Pongwiffy. "Quite the nicest I've ever come across. It just goes to show that they're not all shifty.''

Pongwiffy can sometimes be very gullible.

CHAPTER SIX

FLIGHT

Midnight in Witchway Wood. Frost, stars and a full moon. Time for the flight! All over Witchway Wood, Witch clocks are striking twelve. All except Witch Gaga's, which strikes eighteen, gives a piercing scream, makes a muddy cup of coffee, then explodes.

At the same time, twelve Brooms stir, flex their bristles, and do a bit of sweeping just to get the sap moving. Brooms enjoy the coven meetings. A nice long fly followed by a good gossip. What could be nicer? A chance to have a good old moan about their owners horrible habits, the price of a decent mop bucket and the snobbery of hoovers. Lovely.

In Pongwiffy's garden shed, Woody's limp bristles gave a twitch. It stirred, groaning. In some deep part of its being, it sensed that the hour had come and something important was about to happen.

"Thirty seconds past midnight! There you are! She's late!" Pongwiffy fretted to Hugo. "Told you she would be. Oh, hurry up, Sharky, I'm *frozen*."

The two of them were standing shivering in Pongwiffy's nettle patch, scanning the starry sky for their lift. Their breath steamed in the cold air. Hugo's teeth were chattering so hard he could hardly speak.

October was no time to be standing nose deep in nettles at midnight. Any normal Hamster would be thinking about hibernation by now. But Hugo was no normal Hamster.

"Is cold? I not notice," said Hugo. He even managed a casual little shrug.

That gives you an idea of how tough he was. Beneath that cute, fluffy exterior there were muscles of iron. Let other Hamsters have names like Poochy and Tiddles if they liked. That wasn't for Hugo. Hugo had always wanted to be a Witch Familiar, and if realising his life's ambition meant freezing in a nettle patch at midnight, so be it. He just wore a scarf, blew on his paws and endured.

Pongwiffy hopped impatiently from one foot to the other. She had a battered umbrella under one arm and *How To Make Your Party Swing* under the other. Her pockets were stuffed full of pencil stubs and pieces of paper with scrawled party lists. She had throat spray, because she intended to talk a lot. If there was one thing Pongwiffy liked more than parties, it was planning parties.

"Typical, typical, typical!" she grumbled. "She knows how much tonight means to me. She's doing it on purpose. Oh, bother that stupid Broom. It's quite spoilt my day."

That wasn't quite true. The morning hadn't gone too well, to be sure, but Pongwiffy had quite enjoyed the rest of the day. As soon as she had arrived home, she had hurled the poor unconscious Woody into the garden shed and thrown away the key. She had then recounted the morning's dramatic events to Hugo over several cups of bogwater. She didn't mention Ali Pali. Since parting from him and his toothy smile, she had had one or two misgivings. She had a feeling she may have been rather indiscreet. She had spent the rest of the day reading *How To Make Your Party Swing* and making notes and eating bowl after bowl of warmed over skunk stew. And now, at long last, it was time to go, and Sharkadder was late!

"Ze Broom is comink round, I sink," said Hugo, hearing low clonking noises coming from the garden shed. "Perhaps it feelink better now. Shall I go see?"

"No," rapped Pongwiffy. "Leave it. Stupid thing. Letting me down tonight of all nights. Sharkadder'll be here any minute. She's doing it on purpose to make me suffer. Whatever happens, Hugo, be polite to Dudley until we're airborne."

"Look!" said Hugo suddenly, pointing a tiny paw at the sky. " 'Ere zey come now."

Sharkadder came sailing over the treetops, terribly glamorous in green. Hair, face, dress, cloak, hat, handbag, parasol, boots, everything. All green. She looked like something that had crawled from a rock pool. Slowly and sedately she descended, holding her nose. Dudley perched close behind her, gnawing a chicken bone and looking churlish.

"Ugh," said Sharkadder, touching down in the nettle patch. "That Wall Of Smell of yours is stinking up the sky, Pong. I don't know how you bear it.

Well? What d'you think of the get-up? Do I look nice?"

"Incredible. You've surpassed yourself, Sharky," lied Pongwiffy.

"I have, haven't I?" agreed Sharkadder smugly, batting her eyes and patting her verdant tangles.

"It's a miracle how I managed it considering I now have hardly any make-up to speak of. And we all know who's fault *that* is. Well, hop on, then, if you're coming. Say hello to Hugo, Dudley. If we're all going to share a Broomstick, we might as well try to be civilised."

Dudley was sulking and wouldn't.

"Hello, fat pig cat. How ze fleas?" said Hugo sociably from Pongwiffy's shoulder. Dudley curled his lip and looked the other way, tail twitching.

"You took your time," said Pongwiffy, jumping astride. She felt she could afford to be cocky now she was on board. "Look, there's icicles forming on my hat, we waited so long. If you flew any slower, you'd be going backwards. I hope we're going to fly faster than that. I don't want to be late, you know."

"Look, who's giving who a lift?" said Shark-adder sharply. "It's up to me how fast I fly. I'm not a sky hog like you, Pongwiffy. If there's one thing I can't stand, it's dead flies sticking to my make-up. Any more complaints, and I shan't take you. I'm still not your friend, you know. I'm only doing this under sufferance. Everybody ready for take-off? Right, Broom. Up you go!"

"Hooray!" shrieked Pongwiffy. "Crag Hill, here we come!"

And up they went, Sharkadder's Broom labouring a bit under the extra load.

" 'Tis the 'amster!" hissed Dudley spitefully into Sharkadder's ear. "The Broom can't take its weight. Shall I push it off, Mistress? Just say the word, an' I'll send it to its doom."

"Permission to bite ze fat cat on ze bum Mistress," squeaked Hugo, who had heard.

"Permission denied. Stop making trouble, Hugo," yelled Pongwiffy above the wind. "We're guests on this Broom, remember? Look! The others! Let's catch them up!"

Sure enough, up ahead, Witches Bendyshanks, Sludgegooey, Scrofula and Ratsnappy were flying in convoy, busily swopping recipes.

"Of course, I expect I'll be asked to make my speciality for the Hallowe'en party," Sludgegooey was saying. "Marshmallows. You know the secret of making marshmallows? Marsh. Plenty of it. Of course, it has to be that real, rich, black, stinky stuff.

Quagmire's no good, is it, Filth? Too scummy. Wrong consistency."

The small Fiend perched on Sludgegooey's shoulder agreed that quagmire was a poor substitute for marsh.

"At a pinch, you can use swamp, but they don't come out so light — oh, hello Sharkadder. What's Pongwiffy doing on your Broomstick?"

"I'm getting a lift," explained Pongwiffy. "My Broom's sick. Stick warp, we think."

"Mine had that once," remarked Scrofula. "It kept shedding sawdust everywhere. What with that and my dandruff and Barry moulting, you couldn't see the floor for weeks. We were snowed in. Had to dig ourselves out with shovels in the end. Messy old business. Remember, Barry?

The bald Vulture hunched behind her nodded sadly.

"Oh, really?" said Pongwiffy. "Shedding sawdust, you say? It's not doing that, is it, Sharky?"

"No," admitted Sharkadder. "I can't say I noticed any sawdust. Plenty of face powder, but no sawdust."

"No sawdust, no stick warp," said Scrofula wisely. "It must be something else. What are the symptoms?"

"Oh — nervousness. Cold sweats. Panic attacks," explained Pongwiffy.

"Attacks people's make-up," chipped in Sharkadder with a bitter sniff.

"Faints a lot," continued Pongwiffy. "That sort of thing."

"Sounds like it's had a shock," remarked Bendyshanks. "Have you tried talking to it?"

"What, in Wood you mean? And use that language spell? No fear," said Pongwiffy. "I've tried kicking it, though."

Everyone agreed that if kicking it didn't work, there was little point in talking to it.

"Have you tried being nice to it?" asked Sludgegooey. "Stroke it. Extra rations. Treats. Kindness and sympathy can work wonders. I heard that somewhere."

"Poppycock!" snapped Ratsnappy. "Discipline, that's what's needed. A good, firm hand. You never see my Broom going sick. It wouldn't dare. Sympathy is not a word in my vocabulary."

"What word isn't in your vocabulary?" enquired a voice, and Witch Greymatter flew up

alongside. She had a newspaper balanced across her stick. She was doing a crossword puzzle, and her Owl, whose name was Specs, sat on her shoulder and studied 4 Across.

"What word isn't in your vocabulary, Ratsnappy?" repeated Greymatter. "Unquestionably it will be in mine. I flatter myself that there are very few words with which I am unfamiliar. Specs and I scour the dictionary every morning, and learn a new one. This morning we learnt VISCID. That means sludgy. Glutinous. Slimy, sticky and gluey."

"Like your skunk stew, Pong," said Sharkadder unkindly, and everybody except Pongwiffy nearly fell off their Broomsticks laughing.

"Very funny," said Pongwiffy, and made a mental note that the minute her transportation troubles were sorted out, she would break friends with Sharkadder. Forever this time.

"Here's another one," continued Greymatter, warming to her subject. "SAGACIOUS. It means wise. Knowledgeable. Intelligent."

"Like you, I suppose," growled Ratsnappy.

"Certainly. I don't want to boast, but it's obvious to everyone that I am the brains in this coven."

"Why?" asked everyone.

"Because I write poetry," explained Greymatter loftily. There was no arguing with that. She did. And very highbrow it was too.

"In fact," went on Greymatter. "In fact, Pongwiffy, I was going to suggest that we have a poetry reading at the Hallowe'en party this year. I've written a few special verses for the occasion."

"Er – I'm not too sure about that, Greymatter," hedged Pongwiffy. "I've got a few ideas of my own about the party this year."

"Like what?" asked Ratsnappy suspiciously.

"Ah ha," said Pongwiffy mysteriously. "Wait and see."

Just then, there came the sound of a horn, followed by a mad, blood-chilling screech.

"Gaga," chorused everyone, and hastily got out of the way.

There was a fierce flapping noise, and Witch Gaga hurtled past like some demented surfer on the crest of a wave. A cloud of squeaking bats flapped adoringly around her head. She was wearing wild rags of red, white and blue, and balloons were attached to her hat. She carried a football rattle in one

hand and a tin trumpet
in the other. She was,
of course, thoroughly
bonkers — but in a
jolly sort of way.

The Witches watched with interest. Gaga was
celebrated for her reckless stunt work.

With a wild cry of "Watch me, girls!" she turned
two mid-air somersaults, which brought her Broom
perilously close to the tip of a pine tree. Unwisely,
she attempted a third, and both she and the Broom
disappeared beneath the foliage, obviously destined
for a spectacular crash landing.

"Seen it," chorused the watching Witches, and
flew on.

In time, more tiny figures on Broomsticks flew
up to join the main convoy. The tubby twin Witches
Agglebag and Bagaggle, violins tucked beneath their
chins. Witch Macabre, whose extra-long tartan
painted Broomstick had to be reinforced so that it
could carry the combined weight of herself, her bagpipes and her Haggis, whose name was Rory.
Grandwitch Sourmuddle and Bonidle were the last to
arrive, because Sourmuddle had forgotten the time
and Bonidle had overslept.

That was it. All thirteen of them. The full ragged,
chattering, squabbling complement, gliding along
towards distant Crag Hill in perfect formation.

CHAPTER SEVEN

GUILT ?

Back in the garden shed, Woody finally came to. It sat up with a great deal of groggy groaning and head clutching. It felt awful. It felt disorientated. Confused. It didn't know what day it was. All it knew was that it was in the shed, the shed was dark, and that it was being ogled by the Rake and the Coal Shovel who had obviously just been talking about it behind its back.

Of course, *we* know what Woody has been through in the past twenty-four hours, and can feel some sympathy. All that talk of Goblins and axes on top of the guilty secret it was carrying. It's not surprising it cracked under the strain.

The Rake and the Shovel didn't know any of this, of course. They stared unsympathetically as Woody lurched over to its bucket and took a long, cold drink. They nudged each other as it splashed water down its stick, took deep, steadying breaths and tried to think straight. What time was it? Come to think of it, what year was it?

"Now you're in it," said the Coal Shovel, who could never resist getting a dig in. "Now you're in trouble. Pongwiffy's furious with you."

"Sssh," muttered the Rake. "We sent it to Coventry, remember?"

"I was just saying," explained the Shovel. "I was

just remarking that now it's in trouble. Missing the flight and that."

Suddenly, Woody remembered everything. The Broomnapping. The Goblins. The Plan. The meeting! Oh no! Of course, it was tonight. Even now its fellow Brooms were on their way to the dreaded Broom Park. Supposing — just supposing — the Goblins actually managed to pull it off? Oh guilt, doom and alarm!

Woody gnawed its twiggy fingers, trying not to think about what might happen to its friends. Friends that it had known since it was a sapling. Friends that it had swept with, wept with, grown with and flown with. Ashley. Little Elmer. Scotty McPine. Roots, Stumpy and all the rest. Good friends. Tried, tested and true friends. Friends who always remembered its birthday.

In an agony of remorse, Woody remembered the most important bit of the Broom Code, which said "A Broom sticks up for its friends." It remembered the Broom anthem, which went

> "O riders of the sky are we!
> We'll sweep away the enemy,
> 'Til all the world exclaims, Oh, See -
> There go the noble Broomsticks."

It was a moving song. It set the sap stirring, and brought tears to the eyes. Woody hummed a bit now. Strong emotion made its voice crack.

"What are you singing for?" enquired the Coal Shovel grumpily. "You've got nothing to sing about.

You're in big trouble, you. Shouldn't be surprised if it wasn't the clothes pegs this time. That'll teach you to mend yer flighty ways.''

(The Coal Shovel and Rake were always unfriendly towards Woody. They were jealous because Woody got out more than they did.)

Woody ignored them and carried on singing, louder now. It had got to the chorus, which was the best bit, the bit about Witch Broomsticks being the greatest thing since sliced bread.

> "All for one and one for all,
> Standing proud and straight and tall.
> Sweeping, swooping, loop the looping,
> Gallant, noble Broo-oom-sticks!"

''It's singing the anthem,'' observed the Rake. ''What's it doing that for?''

Woody was now singing at the top of its voice. Its eyes were glazed, its arm raised in a salute. It was changing. It was growing, straightening, standing tall and proud. It beat its stick in time to the music.

"Feeling better, are we?" sneered the Coal Shovel.

Yes. Woody *was* feeling better. Much, much better. And do you know why? Because it had made a major decision, that's why. It was the anthem that did it. It's impossible not to come over all noble when singing such stirring words. By the time it was half way through the chorus, it knew what it had to do. It would come clean. It would fly after the others, confess everything, sound the alarm, and take the consequences. Even if it meant looking a complete twit.

Still singing, it launched into the air, smashed through the shed window and streaked away, bent on rescue.

"Show off," said the Coal Shovel.

"Fly boy," agreed the Rake. And with a sniff, they both settled down to yet another everlasting game of I Spy.

* * * * *

"A thousand curses!"

A short way away, in Pongwiffy's hovel, Ali Pali heard the crash, snuffed out his candle and froze. It was hard to tell that it was Ali Pali, because he was wearing a gas mask. Besides, the place was in pitch darkness. However, it was indeed him. His carpet bag lay open on Pongwiffy's table. It contained various curious items. Bottles of cheap perfume. Discontinued lines of strong aftershave. Tins of air freshener. A megaphone. A cash register. Coloured flags. Crayons. A folding tent. It was amazing how it all fitted in.

After the crash came the sound of tinkling glass, followed by a sort of whoosh. After that, silence. Ali Pali waited a moment, then gave a shrug, re-lit his candle and continued to be up to no good.

CHAPTER EIGHT

THE MEETING

On Crag Hill, a cheery fire was blazing. Witches and Familiars milled about, chattering and gossiping and greedily eying the sandwiches which were piled high on trestle tables. The sandwiches were always the highlight of these affairs. The trouble was, no one was allowed to eat them until coven business had been attended to. Which explains why the formal part of coven meetings always tends to be short.

The formal part hadn't yet started. Everyone was just hanging around, filling in time. Agglebag and Bagaggle practised a new duet on their violins. Ratsnappy and Scrofula picked holes in each other's knitting. Every so often, there would be a little flash of light as one of the Witches demonstrated a new spell, followed by shouts of admiration or loud ridicule, depending on how impressive it was. Further up the hill in the Broom Park, the Broomsticks, parked and promptly forgotten, talked amongst themselves.

Pongwiffy was very much in evidence, acting all mysterious about the wonderful ideas she had for the forthcoming party and talking loudly about her Broom troubles. Much to Sharkadder's disgust, she had gathered quite a crowd. All Witches consider themselves experts in such matters, and everyone had an opinion. Sharkadder was particularly annoyed when Pongwiffy acted out the bit where the Broom trod on Dudley's tail and got a huge laugh. Dudley was so upset, he had to go behind a bush and bite on a rock.

"Not funny, Pongwiffy!" howled Sharkadder.

"Oh, poo. Where's your sense of humour, Sharky? Now, as I was saying. . ."

But then:

"Quiet please!" called a shrill, quavering old voice. "If we're all ready, I'd like to call this meeting to order. Witches, kindly be upstanding. Pass me my umbrella, Snoop. If they don't stop yapping, Macabre, give 'em a blast on your bagpipes."

The voice belonged to Grandwitch Sourmuddle, the mistress of the Witchway coven. Two hundred years old, with a shocking memory. Firelight glinted on her spectacles, and on the pitchfork of the small, exasperated Demon who perched on her shoulder, forked tail draped around her neck like a long scarf. His name was Snoop, and he was Sourmuddle's Familiar.

Witch Macabre raised her pipes to her lips with a threatening gesture. Rory, her Haggis, gave a warning moo. Immediately, the gossip and chatter died down. Knitting was put away, noses blown and coughs stifled. Witches and Familiars stood to attention. Those who had remembered umbrellas opened them. The rest stood with hunched shoulders, looking resigned.

"Hail, Witches!" piped the Grandwitch.

"Hail!" came the response. As always, a small cloud came buzzing through the sky and delivered a short, sharp burst of hailstones before busily whizzing off again.

"I declare the boring, formal bit of this meeting open," announced Sourmuddle, folding her umbrella. "Right. Park yer bums."

There was an immediate scramble for a warm spot in front of the fire. After a great deal of jostling and pushing, they were all finally sitting comfortably. (Or in Gaga's case, hanging comfortably from a nearby tree.) Pongwiffy made sure she was in the middle of the front row. Hugo climbed to the rim of her hat, where he could see better. On one side of them sat Sharkadder and Dudley. On the other slumped Witch Bonidle and her Sloth, who was acting as a pillow. As usual, they were both fast asleep. A half eaten apple dangled from Bonidle's limp hand.

Pongwiffy pinched it and finished it off for her. That's Witch behaviour for you.

Scrofula stuck her hand in the air.

"Excuse me, Sourmuddle. Can Barry and I be excused? Neither of us are feeling too well. If you don't mind, we'd like to take our share of the sandwiches and go home. I've got a sore throat, and Barry's moulting again, aren't you Barry?"

She nudged the sad, bald vulture, and he gave an obliging cough.

"Not likely," said Sourmuddle. "You're going to stay here and suffer with the rest of us. Yes, Sharkadder? What's the matter with you?"

"Grandwitch Sourmuddle, I've got a complaint about Pongwiffy. Do you know what she did? Or rather, what she let her Broom do. She..."

"Later, Sharkadder, later. You know that complaints about Pongwiffy come under Any Other Business. First things first. We are here tonight to discuss ... er ... we are here to ... what are we here to discuss, Snoop?"

There was a general sigh.

"The Hallowe'en Party," Snoop reminded her wearily. "I've told you a thousand times."

"Yes, yes, I knew all the time, I was just testing you. Find the coven account book, will you? And somebody wake up Bonidle. I can't hear myself think with her snoring like that."

Snoop raised his eyes to heaven, slid down and rummaged about in a black plastic bin liner. It was full of all kinds of junk. Spell books, wands, magical potions, crystal balls and the odd toad or two were all jumbled up with a flask of hot soup, gum boots, cough medicine, corn plasters and an extra scarf for the flight home. Sourmuddle liked to be prepared. Finally, a dog-eared old exercise book came to light.

Meanwhile, Pongwiffy helpfully tried to wake Bonidle, who, you will remember, was fast asleep, head on Sloth. (The Sloth, incidentally doesn't have a name. Bonidle is too lazy to think of one, and the Sloth is too tired to care.)

Pongwiffy's method of awakening the sleeping beauty was to administer a sharp dig in the ribs with the handle of her umbrella. Accidentally on purpose, she managed to poke Sharkadder up the nose with the sharp end. For Sharkadder, this was the final straw. The uneasy truce between them was broken.

"Idiot!" hissed Sharkadder. "That's it! As of now, I am no longer your friend! You can walk home."

"If I walk home, you don't get to judge the fancy dress," threatened Pongwiffy. "And you can't be in it either," she added.

"Be quiet, Pongwiffy and Sharkadder," scolded Grandwitch Sourmuddle. "This is an important meeting. It's essential that we pay attention. We have to discuss the arrangements for the party."

"Is that all?" complained Witch Macabre. "What aboot a fight? Can we noo have a friendly wee fisticuffs, then?"

"Sorry to disappoint you, Macabre, but there's no fighting tonight."

Macabre went into a deep sulk, and Rory pawed the ground with a frustrated hoof. (Rory is interesting. Macabre insists that he is the only live Haggis in existence. Looking at him, that is probably just as well. Rory has a great deal of shaggy fur and a daft-looking fringe which hangs over his eyes. He is so interesting, he deserves a whole book to himself - but there isn't enough room in this one.)

"Pongwiffy?" called Sourmuddle. "I've got a horrible feeling it's your turn to organise the Hallowe'en party this year."

"It certainly is, Sourmuddle!" yelled Pongwiffy, leaping to her feet, sticking her arm in the air, quivering with keenness. "This year's party will be the best yet!"

"Wrong," said Sourmuddle, opening the account book. "Terrible news, I'm afraid. We can't afford a party this year. We're out of funds. We spent the last of our money on that coach trip to Sludgehaven-on-Sea."

This announcement was greeted with loud

moans. Pongwiffy couldn't believe her ears.

"*No party?*" she shrieked. "But it's my *turn*, Sourmuddle. Of course we must have a party. I've got loads of wonderful ideas!"

"Well, all right, perhaps no party at all is going a bit far," relented Sourmuddle. "But we'll have to cut out a few things. Like the balloons, the funny hats, the barbecue, the band, the prizes, the cake, the party bags, the..."

"Stop, stop! You're cutting everything out. There's nothing left!" wailed Pongwiffy.

"Yes there is. We can bring sandwiches, like we did tonight. And we can still sit and cackle around the bonfire. I'm sorry, Pongwiffy. I know you think you're the world's best organiser, though I can't think why. But if we haven't got any money, there's not a lot we can do, is there? Right. Meeting over. Let's eat."

The consensus seemed to be that this was a jolly good idea. There was a general stirring and rising and scrabbling about for wands and handbags. Until....

"Hold it right there!" Pongwiffy, of course. "Certainly we must have a proper party! Where's our pride? Do we not have a reputation to uphold? Are we not the best party givers this side of the Misty Mountains? Of course we are. Sandwiches! Cackling around bonfires! Hah!"

"What's wrong with cackling around bonfires?" demanded Ratsnappy fiercely. "We've always cackled around bonfires on Hallowe'en. It's tradition.''

"Aye!" agreed Macabre. "We've heard your crackpot ideas befoor, Pongwiffy. Ah'm all foor tradition."

"Nonsense," said Pongwiffy. "Don't be such old stick in the muds. Listen, I've got an idea for this year's party which'll really put this coven on the map. It comes from this wonderful book which I found and just happen to have right here."

With a bold gesture, she held the crumbling edition of *How To Make Your Party Swing* above her head.

"Listen!" she shrieked with the glassy-eyed conviction of the converted. "Listen! What about *this* for an idea, then! FANCY DRESS!"

A long silence. Apart from Sharkadder, blank faces. Nobody had ever heard of such a thing before. The trouble was, nobody wanted to be the first to admit it.

"Not that it matters, as we can't afford it anyway – but what's Fancy Dress?" asked Sourmuddle, who was too old to care about seeming silly. Everyone breathed a sigh of relief.

"Ah! Well, we dress up as someone or something else, you see," explained Pongwiffy. "It can be anything. And there'll be a prize for the best costume."

"I knew that," Sharkadder told everyone knowledgeably. "It's a very modern idea, actually."

"When you say it can be anything, what exactly do you mean?" enquired Greymatter. "You mean, a queen or a penguin or a bar of soap?"

"Exactly right, Greymatter," beamed Pongwiffy. "You've got the idea. We could dress up as stone age cavewomen if we liked. In sabre-toothed tiger skins."

"A bit chilly," pointed out Sourmuddle. "Crag Hill's not the warmest of spots in October. I've got three vests on now, and an extra cardi. Besides, where am I supposed to lay me hands on a sabre toothed tiger's skin? They're extinct, aren't they?"

Pongwiffy sighed. This was going to be an uphill struggle.

"No, no, Sourmuddle, I just said cavewomen as an example. You might want to be something completely different. A Gypsy. Robin Hood. A Pencil. A Princess. Anything you like. You choose. See?"

There was another long silence, while everybody thought about it. Fancy Dress, eh? Wearing something other than rags for a change. Hmm. It took a bit of getting used to. On the other hand, it might be a bit of fun. Especially if there was a prize.

"That's all very well, Pongwiffy," said Bendyshanks, "but we can't even afford to buy a cake. Where do we get the money for costumes, may I ask?"

"I'll get it!" promised Pongwiffy rashly. "I'll get the money, don't you worry. I've got the rubbish for the bonfire, I might as well do everything else. Don't worry, girls, not only will we have a party this year, but it'll be the best one yet! Just wait till you hear the rest of my ideas. What I propose is this. . ."

But she got no further. Instead, there came an interruption. There was a whistling noise from high above, and something long and thin came hurtling out of the sky, straight as an arrow, whizz, bang, down into their midst.

CHAPTER NINE

COMMUNICATION PROBLEMS

Who was this unexpected visitor? Woody, of course.
Bent on its errand of mercy.

"Oh no," muttered Pongwiffy to Hugo. "It's
going to show me up again. I just know it."

"It's that wretched Broom again!" cried Shark-
adder. "I thought you said you locked it in the shed,
Pongwiffy. What's it doing here? Look, everyone,
Pongwiffy's Broom! It's flown here all on it's own,
and that's against the rules, isn't it, Sourmuddle?
That deserves three black marks at least."

"Objection!" protested Pongwiffy. "It's not *my*
fault it's here is it? Home! Home this minute,
Broom."

This brought a storm of protest. Nobody wanted to lose the Broom just yet. All Witches love talking about illnesses, especially operations. They consider themselves experts at diagnosing faults in their equipment, whether it be wands, cauldrons or Broomsticks. Everyone had a pet theory about Pongwiffy's ailing Broom. Suggestions ranged from high sap pressure, to Acute Nerves Brought On By Living With Pongwiffy. They were all terribly keen to observe the patient in the flesh – or wood, rather.

Besides, Pongwiffy's Broom was really most entertaining. Amongst other things, it was licking Pongwiffy's boots, would you believe!

"Sharkadder's quite right, Pongwiffy," said Sourmuddle. "That Broom shouldn't be out on it's own. No Flying Without A Witch. It says so clearly in the rule book."

"But, Sourmuddle, I left it in the shed!" protested Pongwiffy. "It's not my fault if it followed me. Oh, do stop it, Broom! Down! You're behaving like an idiot!"

She was right. Woody was. It had finished boot licking, and was now jumping about like a badly trained puppy. It was making short, agitated little runs, pointing urgently up the hill, beckoning, then coming back to tug at her cardigan sleeve. Pongwiffy was terribly embarrassed, and smacked it hard on the stick.

"It wants to go walkies," remarked Bendyshanks with a smirk. "Look! It thinks it's a dog!"

"Give it a bone, Pongwiffy!" jeered Sludgegooey to general laughter.

"Woof woof," barked Agglebag and Bagaggle, rocking with the giggles.

"No control," sneered Ratsnappy. "Firm handling, that's what Brooms need."

"Excuse me, Grandvitch Sourmuddle," said Hugo. "I sink zis Broom is tryink to tell us sumpsink. It got big, important news for us, zis Broom. I am sure of it."

"Well, we can find out soon enough," remarked Sourmuddle. "Use that language spell, Pongwiffy, and ask it. You know. Zithery, zithery zoom. . ."

"Never," said Pongwiffy firmly. "Ever tried using that spell, Sourmuddle?"

"Well, yes, I see what you mean," admitted Sourmuddle. "Awful side-effects. Any volunteers to speak Wood? In the cause of medical science?"

There were none, of course. Even in the cause of medical science, nobody could face those awful side-effects. One or two lost interest altogether, and began to drift towards the sandwiches.

Poor Woody. What an anti-climax. It had come all this way, perfectly prepared to do the honourable thing and take the consequences. But it had forgotten one critical thing. Nobody could speak Wood.

"Can it write?" enquired Scrofula, not very hopefully.

"Only in Wood," said Pongwiffy. So that was no good.

"I have a suggestion. It could tap out a message in morse code!"

That was Witch Greymatter. At the time, it seemed like a good idea.

"Broom!" ordered Pongwiffy sternly. "Kindly take yourself over to that tree and tap out whatever you have to say in morse code."

At last! They were making some headway! Everyone crowded round and listened hard while Woody carefully tapped out the message on a tree trunk. DANGER. BE PREPARED. GOBLINS PLANNING TO RAID BROOM PARK TONIGHT. FORGOT TO MENTION EARLIER. SORRY. MY FAULT. YOURS SINCERELY, WOODY.

Sadly, when it finally reached the end, it turned out that no one could understand morse code anyway. It was all most terribly frustrating for everybody.

"I know! It can act it out!"

That suggestion came from Filth, Sludgegooey's Fiend. "You know, like in charades. One word at a time."

"What d'you think, Broom?" asked Pongwiffy. "Think you can do it?"

Woody thought it unlikely. It had never thought of itself as an actor. But desperate measures were called for. It held up one twiggy finger.

"First word," chorused everyone, clustering round. This was more like it. This was fun. This was entertainment. Next to eating, casting spells and talking about illnesses, if there's one thing Witches enjoy, it's charades.

Woody hesitated for a moment. Then, it made a sudden sideways lunge at Witch Scrofula, who happened to be wearing a bright red scarf. Scrofula gave a squawk of protest as her favourite neck warmer was snatched away and waved furiously in the air.

"Scarf," said Greymatter. "It's trying to tell us it's got a sore throat. That's obvious."

Wild with frustration, Woody shook its head and flapped the scarf some more.

"It wants to do some knitting," suggested Sharkadder. "It's bored and feels like a bit of a knit. Looks like one, too," she added unkindly.

"Leave it alone, Sharkadder," said Pongwiffy. "It's doing its best."

"It obvious vat it tryink to show," said Hugo, who was very good at charades. "It try to show ze colour red. Red for danger. Right, Broom?"

Woody nodded emotionally. It could have wept with gratitude. Now they were getting somewhere. Everyone cheered, and Hugo took a bow. Scrofula snatched back her scarf, and sullenly wound it round her neck.

"Okay. Ze first vord is danger. Zis ve know. Vat next?"

Woody thought for a moment. This next one was going to stretch its talent to the utmost limits. First, it cupped its ear.

"Sounds like," chorused one and all, caught up in the spirit of the thing. Encouraged, Woody suddenly winced, as though its bristles hurt. It then began to walk very slowly, swaying from side to side. We know what it was doing, don't we? Hobbling. Because hobbling sounds vaguely like Goblin, and that was all it could think of.

"It's limping!" yelled Filth, Sludegooey's Fiend. "What sounds like limp?"

"Chimp! There's a wild chimp on the loose?" guessed Witch Ratsnappy, suddenly inspired. But Woody was shaking its head. That wasn't it. They all thought again.

"Shuffling?"

"Blisters?"

"Athlete's foot? Bad leg?"

The suggestions kept coming, all wrong, wrong, hopelessly wrong. Woody was getting near the end of its tether. Its fevered imagination conjured up the sound of far crashings and muffled cries coming from the direction of the Broom Park, which was clearly under attack *right now*. It simply *had* to make these idiot Witches understand. Desperately, it thought of its own personal motto — "Stick with it" — and tried hobbling harder...

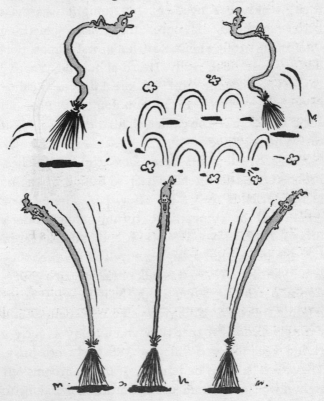

CHAPTER TEN

THE RAID

So. What *was* happening in the Broom Park?

Not a lot.

The Brooms were propped against various trees, engaged in deep discussion. They always enjoyed their weekly get-togethers, but tonight was even better because, for once, they had something interesting to talk about. Real, hot news! Almost bordering on scandal, really. Heard about old Woody? No. What? Some sort of breakdown. Really? Oooooh. Yep. Too ill to fly. You don't say! Poor old stick. Chucked in the garden shed, did you say? Tut tut. What a shame.

Eagerly, they compared notes. Unlike Witches, Brooms are rather a tender-hearted bunch when one of their friends feels a bit below par. There was a great deal of sympathetic tutting. Sharkadder's Broom, Ashley (Woody's best friend), shed a tear or two and proposed buying a get well card which they would all sign. There was talk of taking up a collection and sending along a bunch of flowers. Sourmuddle's Broom, Stumpy, went one better, and daringly proposed that they should pay Woody a flying visit. Now. While the Witches were busy. They were sure to be hours yet. If the Brooms left right now, there would just be time to whizz along to

Woody's shed and pay their poor old mate a lightning visit. Maybe stop off somewhere and buy a few grapes. Surprise surprise! Bet you didn't expect us, etc. All right, so it wasn't strictly allowed, but in the circumstances, surely ...? Besides, Woody's illness sounded quite spectacular. Though they wouldn't admit it, they were all keen to have a good old gawp.

The snap of a twig, a muffled sneeze. Oh dear. Who's that creeping up under cover of the bushes? They were so concerned and caring, those Brooms, so caught up in their friend's sorry plight that they didn't notice they were being sneaked up on by...

Goblins! Yes. It's them all right. Incredible as it might seem, Plugugly, Slopbucket, Lardo, Hog, Sproggit, Stinkwart and Eyesore have actually made it! They have walked on tiptoe all the way from Goblin Territory to Crag Hill. It has taken them hours and hours, but they are here. As far as they are concerned, they are about to carry out the biggest Broomnapping in the whole of history. Of course, it all depends on the success of Plugugly's Plan.

The Goblins are really trying hard with this one, and to give credit where it's due, they haven't done too badly at all so far. A few minor details have gone wrong, but they've got the most important things right. For a start, they have remembered to come.

They also have the correct evening. They have even made an effort to disguise themselves. Plugugly is wearing a false nose, Lardo and Hog have done things with paper bags, and the others are got up as bushes.

They are doing other things right too. They are attempting to blend into the shadows. They are downwind of their prey. They have a secret password, which none of them can pronounce. The word is UNPRONOUNCEABLE.

In the dark, it's difficult to tell friend from foe, so they keep whispering it, just to be on the safe side. In between attempting to pronounce unpronounceable, they are making the sort of noises that they feel small woodland creatures might make, in case the Brooms get suspicious. They are armed to the teeth with everything you might possibly need for a mass Broomnapping. Sacks, ropes, nets, gags, pitchforks, string, whistles, megaphones, a bag of humbugs and a large box of matches. Ten out of ten for effort.

It was a terribly tense time for the Goblins. They never, ever managed to do anything right, and they all felt the strain. It would be so nice if, just once, a Goblin Plan worked properly – but it was always the same. Whatever they attempted – be it a simple hunting trip, a raid on Pongwiffy's rubbish tip, or tying up their boot laces – they always seemed to mess it up. Plugugly was particularly nervous, because it was his very own Plan.

It went like this.

1. Creep up in disguise
2. Capture Brooms
3. Take broooms Home in Cart
5. Hide Broooms!

This was very detailed for a Goblin Plan and Plugugly was rightfully proud of it. He normally just fell in with other people's plans, but this one he had thought up all by himself. That made him the leader. So he was responsible for attending to the details. For checking the equipment. For telling everyone what to do. For making sure they did it. No wonder he was nervous.

It was good, though, being the leader. Plugugly was enjoying the novelty of it all. When he realised that he could boss people around, he told Sproggit to oil the wheels of the cart. The one they would use to carry the broomnapping equipment to Crag Hill and their victims back to Goblin Territory.

That was the first thing that went wrong. Sprog-git forgot. So the cart squeaked most irritatingly as the Goblins tiptoed all the way from Goblin Territory to Crag Hill – and believe me, that's a very long way. Also, a squeaking cart rather tends to spoil the element of surprise. So they decided to abandon it at the foot of Crag Hill and carry the equipment the rest of the way.

The disguises hadn't really worked that well. Everyone and everything they met along the way recognised them instantly and fell about laughing. That was disappointing. However, Plugugly consoled himself with the thought that they hadn't yet mucked up anything major. Part 1 of the Plan – Creeping Up In Disguise – was now complete. Time for Part 2, which was Capture Brooms. The Goblins had rehearsed this bit over and over again. At the signal – which was Plugugly shouting "Ready, Steady, Go!" – they would all leap out with sticks and ropes and so on, grab the Brooms, wrestle them to the ground, and bind and gag them.

This bit of the plan was hopeless. It had more holes in than the nets the Goblins had brought. They never got it right in rehearsals, when there weren't even any real Brooms. For a start, Plugugly never managed to say Ready, Steady, Go! in the right order, so the Goblins never managed to leap at the same time. Somebody always tripped over. Nobody was quite sure what to do once he'd wrestled his Broom to the ground. Supposing it wrestled back? Brooms were as slippery as eels, if Pongwiffy's was anything to go by. There they were, then, hiding behind trees and bushes, waiting for the signal, feeling horribly nervous. Plugugly adjusted his false nose, licked his lips, and tried to remember the order of the words. How did it go again?

"Reddysteddygo," muttered Plugugly to himself. "Reddysteddygo. Dat's it. Right den. 'Ere goes. Er... "REDDYGOSTEDDY!"

Poor Plugugly. The most important thing he'd ever had to do, and he mucked it up. The rest of the Goblins stared at each other, wondering whether they should leap now or make Plugugly do it again and get it right. Sproggit, Slopbucket and Lardo hesitantly leapt. Hog, Eyesore and Stinkwort remained where they were. Sproggit, Slopbucket and Lardo ran back again, red with embarrassment. It was a farce. But it didn't matter either way. Because at exactly the moment that Plugugly mucked it up, the Brooms suddenly took off! Just like that, of their own accord. No warning, straight up, all together. Once airborne, they hovered for a moment – then, as one, they turned and flew off in a southerly direction. They were off to visit their ol' mate Woody. They didn't even know that they'd been sneaked up on, let alone leapt out at.

The Goblins watched, open-mouthed, as the Brooms flew away. There was a long silence. Then...

"Typical," remarked young Sproggit with a shrug. Which it was.

CHAPTER ELEVEN

A STATE OF EMERGENCY

Meanwhile, back down the hill, the game of charades continued. Woody's performance was reaching dizzying heights. Before or since, no Broom has ever hobbled quite as convincingly and sincerely as Woody hobbled that night. It had found a stick, and was using it as a crutch. It winced at every step. Desperation lent real strength and majesty to its performance. So it wasn't surprising that, at long last, Hugo got it!

" 'Obbling!'' squeaked Hugo. "Ze Broom is 'obbling!''

Woody wept with relief.

"Oh, well done, Hugo,'' said Pongwiffy, patting him on the back. "Now then. What sounds like hobbling? Bobbling, cobbling — Hey! Gobbling, of course! And gobbling sounds like Goblin. I knew it! Remember, Sharky? It came over all weird earlier when we mentioned Goblins. I'm right, aren't I, Broom?''

Drained by its performance, Woody gave a weak nod, and there was general relief all round. Everyone was having a great time. Well, not quite everyone. Sharkadder was annoyed because Pongwiffy was the centre of attention yet again. Dudley was vexed because Hugo had been the shining star of this particular game of charades. Macabre and Rory were missing. Bonidle was asleep, and a few of the Familiars had lost interest and were talking amongst themselves. But apart from *that*, everybody was having a great time.

"Right," Pongwiffy summed up, "we have Danger, Goblins. Now we have to get the next bit. You've done all right so far, Broom. We've seen some brilliant acting tonight, eh, girls?"

Scattered applause. Woody gave a weak bow.

"Concentrate, Broom," urged Hugo. "Ve need to know *vhere* and *vat* is zis danger of vich you speak. Please act out ze next vord."

But Woody never got the chance. A sound of galloping hooves came from the trees and Macabre, mounted on Rory, crashed into the glade. Her hat was over one eye, and she was bursting with importance. She was shouting and whooping and waving something triumphantly on high.

It was a grubby Goblin bobble hat!

Macabre pulled on the reigns sharply, and Rory skidded to a halt.

"Treachery!" howled Macabre. "Treachery and skulduggery! The Brooms ha' bin nicked, every last one. We bin robbed, girrrls. And d'ye ken who by? Goblins, that's who. Look! Look what Ah foond!"

Macabre speared the evidence on the end of her bagpipes and waved it under people's noses.

Alarm and consternation! Cries of anger, flapping of wings, flexing of claws, gnashing of teeth, shaking of fists. Panic, accusations, and a lot of running around and shouting. Two cases of hysterics, and three of fainting. Macabre wanted to form a posse. Greymatter wanted to take a vote. Gaga fell out of her tree. Agglebag and Bagaggle came over all funny and took turns fanning each other. It wasn't often that such dramatic events occurred during coven meetings, and the Witches wanted to get their money's worth. In the midst of it all, Pongwiffy was leaping up and down in a ripe royal fury, giving Woody a piece of her mind.

"Idiot! Nincompoop! Stupid, dozy, wooden-brained plank-head! I see it all now. You got caught by Goblins, didn't you? That's where you were all that time when you went missing. You overheard their plans, didn't you? You knew all along about this, didn't you? You great sap. You useless cleaning utensil. Why didn't you tell me before? Twig brain!"

Woody hung its head and said nothing. From great actor to useless cleaning utensil in ten easy insults. Oh, the shame of it all. It was now a broken Broom who deserved everything that Pongwiffy threw at it.

"All right, all right, that's enough. No need to get carried away. Calm down, everyone!" ordered Grandwitch Sourmuddle severely. "What's all the fuss? It's only Goblins. And Goblins are bungling idiots, remember? They don't even have Magic. Watch me. I'll get our Brooms back with a flick of me wand. Where's me wand, Snoop?"

"In your hand," pointed out Snoop.

"Just testing. Right, then. Watch the sky for returning Broomsticks. *Head of beer and tail of deer, make our Broomsticks reappear!*"

And Sourmuddle gave her wand a little flick. Now, at this point, something impressive should have happened. A rumble of thunder, maybe, and a flash of lightning. At the very least, green smoke. The night sky should then have swarmed with prodigal Broomsticks. A glad reunion should have followed. The Goblins would have been captured and dealt with most severely. Then, everyone could have eaten the sandwiches and gone home.

Not so this time. Everyone was eagerly craning upwards, but nothing happened. Well, that's not quite right. What happened was that Sourmuddle's wand gave a feeble little phut, sprayed a few green sparks then went limp.

"That's worrying," said Grandwitch Sourmuddle, flopping it about like a length of liquorice. "Only had it serviced recently. Hmm. I wonder. Everyone had better inspect their equipment."

Alarmed Witches scrabbled in their pockets and handbags. It's surprising how much a Witch can get in her handbag. Wands, bells, books, candles, crystal balls, even fold-up cauldrons were produced, along with a load of dirty tissues, small frogs, toothless combs, photographs of loved ones and fluffy old half-sucked boiled sweets. There was a lot of flicking and muttering and peering and little exclamations of dismay.

"Sourmuddle! My wand's gone wonky too!" shouted Pongwiffy importantly. "Look, it's all floppy, see? Just like yours." Nobody took any notice. Pongwiffy's equipment seldom did work, mainly because she never cleaned it.

"I don't know about you lot, but my crystal ball's up the creek," said Sourmuddle. "Might as well try to see into a cow pat."

Crystal ball owners excitedly agreed that theirs were displaying the same mysterious symptoms.

"And guess what! The pages of my Pocket Spell Book are all stuck up, with mysterious invisible glue," cried Sludgegooey. "It's usually egg," she explained to anyone who was interested.

"Oh no! My best wishbone's snapped!"

"Look, everybody, I can't make little green explosions any more! See? I snapped my fingers and nothing happened."

"I don't know about you lot, but my brain's gone blank. I can't even remember the ingredients for a basic brew!"

It was true. Bells wouldn't ring, books wouldn't open and candles wouldn't light. Brains had gone blank of the simplest spells. There wasn't a stiff Wand to be seen. Wand droop was the order of the day.

"Sabotage!" hissed Sourmuddle thrillingly.

"Sabotage, shinnanigans and hanky panky. You know what, Witches? There's another Power at work, blocking ours. I've come across this sort of thing before. Some cheeky upstart has got hold of our top secret Magic code numbers. The ones we're never supposed to divulge on pain of being lowered into a well and pelted with bad eggs. All right, you lot, who's been giving out inside information? Come on, come on, it's obvious that one of you has been shooting her mouth off."

That was when Pongwiffy had a rather nasty coughing fit. It was so bad, she had to go behind a tree for a moment.

"Oh well, there's only one thing to do," continued Sourmuddle. "I hereby declare an Official State Of Emergency."

There was a loud cheer. Official State Of Emergency, eh? They didn't have one of those very often. It sounded terribly exciting.

"Basically, girls, we're in a bit of a fix. No Magic. No transport. It's obvious somebody's up to no good behind our backs! But who?"

"Booo! Just wait till we get our hands on 'em!"

"Grrrr!"

There was a lot of enthusiastic shouting. Pongwiffy got over her coughing fit, stepped casually out from her tree, and shouted louder than anyone.

"Why did you go behind that tree just then, Pongwiffy?" asked Sharkadder, sidling up.

"Mind your own business," said Pongwiffy. "Grrr! Boo! Down with cheeky upstarts!"

"Who? Who?" pondered Sourmuddle. "Who's got the nerve to mess with Witches on the run up to Hallowe'en?"

Everyone thought hard. It wasn't likely to be the Wizards, who were far too snooty. Likewise the Skeletons. The Ghouls didn't have the nerve. The Goblins didn't have the brains. Although there was the bobble hat, of course. . . .

"I'm fed up wi' all this talk," announced Macabre, who was a Witch of action. "I'm goin' back tay the Broom Park tay look for more clues." And she mounted and rode off.

"Oh well, there's nothing else for it," decided Sourmuddle. "Where are you, Pongwiffy?"

"Me? Why? What d'you want me for?" demanded Pongwiffy, terribly flustered to be picked on.

"You'll just have to fly off and find out what's going on," explained Sourmuddle. "You're the only one with transport, remember? So it's up to you to sort it out. Besides, if you had proper control over your Broom none of this would have happened. So I hold you personally responsible for getting our Brooms back. Off you go. And don't take all night about it."

"What – all on my own?" complained Pongwiffy, glancing hopefully at Sharkadder. Sharkadder tossed her hair, linked her arm in Sludgegooey's and purposely turned her back.

"Don't be such a baby, Pongwiffy," said Sour-muddle, impatient to get at the sandwiches. "Off you go. One Witch is more than a match for Goblins. Even you."

"But my wand's not working and my Broom might not be well enough to fly and I don't even know where to start looking and we haven't finished discussing the party . . ."

"Stop making excuses," said Sourmuddle. "We're in a State Of Emergency. It's hardly the time to think about parties, is it? Hardly the time to think about enjoying ourselves. Hey, Agglebag! Grab one of those spiderspread sandwiches for me, will you? Now, buzz off, Pongwiffy, and don't come back without those Broomsticks. Right girls. After three. When you're smi-ling, when you're smi-ling. . ."

And in seconds, the trestle tables were under attack and Pongwiffy, Hugo and the disgraced Woody were left quite alone. Nobody offered to accompany them on their mission. Sharkadder was tucking in without even glancing in Pongwiffy's direction.

Oh well. There was nothing else for it. Grimly, Pongwiffy grabbed Woody. It shied nervously, then held steady as Pongwiffy clambered aboard.

"Vere ve go first, Mistress?" asked Hugo, scuttling up to the rim of her hat.

"Up," said Pongwiffy irritably. "Where else?"

Desperate to please, Woody went up.

☆ ❀ ☆ ❀ ☆ 🌙
CLEANING UP ✦

How Ali Pali ever managed to do it in the time will always remain a mystery. You had to hand it to him. When it came to transformations, that Genie was a genius.

The Dump had been taken over and changed beyond all recognition. It had been spruced up and tartified. It now looked like a sort of cross between a rubbish tip and an oriental fair ground. It had an exotic, Aladdinish sort of allure. It was brilliantly illuminated. Coloured magic lanterns. Fairy lights. Bunting. Flags. That sort of thing.

Ali Pali obviously believed in heavy advertising. There were posters tacked up on trees all over Witchway Wood, advertising the event in huge, screaming letters.

TONIGHT! GRAND RAID ON RUBBISH DUMP! EVERYTHING MUST GO! FIVE QUID ONLY FOR TEN MINUTES UNINTERRUPTED LOOTING. BRING YOUR FRIENDS. HAVE FUN! WALL OF SMELL DISMANTLED COURTESY OF GENIE ENTERPRISES.

Yes, indeed, the Wall Of Smell had gone. The tip now smelt strongly of the antidote (the main ingredient of which was a cheap eastern hair oil called Desert Pong).

At the entrance, a striped awning had been erected. Inside, Ali Pali sat cross-legged on a pile of cushions. He was smoking a large cigar and stuffing fivers into a till. He was further equipped with a megaphone and a very fancy pocket watch which he consulted regularly. His carpet bag lay at his feet. A large ruby was flashing on one of the medallions

around his neck (otherwise you would never have known that he was simultaneously working very complicated Magic. Erecting a barrier on all incoming spells from Crag Hill to be precise. It's all rather technical and hard to understand unless you're a paid up member of the Magic Circle).

A long queue stretched far back into the woods. It consisted of the usual crowd. A languid group of Skeletons; a gang of Ghouls, behaving like louts as always; the local chapter of the Hell's Gnomes; a bevy of Banshees and a troupe of Trolls; several hairy types you couldn't really put a name to. Everyone clutched handbills saying *All You Can Carry For A Fiver* and wore expressions of barely containable glee. They had been itching to get their hands on Pongwiffy's rubbish for weeks.

Two buskers entertained the waiting hordes. A tap-dancing Gnome with a banjo attempted to drown out a Leprechaun who sang a sad song about his grey haired ol' mudder. Every so often they would stop to bawl insults at each other and pass their hats along.

Once inside, the fun really started. There was better class entertainment for a start. A sinister figure with a paper bag over his head(?) turned the handle of a barrel organ. A tall, quiet chap with a bolt through his neck played the spoons. An enterprising Fiend was selling commemorative badges saying "I Raided Pong's Dump" followed by the date. A lipsticky gnome in big earrings had taken over Pongwiffy's garden shed and turned it into a fortune-telling booth where she dished out lashings of doom to anyone fool enough to poke his nose in. In order to give herself room she had turfed out a rusty old rake and an ancient coal shovel she'd found cluttering up the place.

There were refreshments too. As the ultimate insult, Pongwiffy's hovel had been turned into a tea hut. *Teas* said the sign over the door. *The Management Accepts No Responsibility* said the small print. Pongwiffy's very own kitchen table and chairs had been placed outside, and two Yetis in filthy aprons moved around with a tray, wiping up spills with *one of Pongwiffy's very own cardigans*!

Next to the tea hut, there was the inevitable hot frogs stall. The hot frogs were proving rather more popular than the vegetarian alternatives – a choice of fungus burgers or curried nettles served on a bed of lightly toasted pine needles.

But the main attraction, of course, was The Rubbish. Perfect bonfire fodder. It made you drool. It made you want to dance and sing. It made you go a bit funny in the head. All that lovely rubbish, just sitting there waiting to be stolen. Yipppeeeee!

Once the punters were inside the gate, a sort of rubbish fever came over them. They raced madly for the teetering piles, falling on choice items with wild triumphant cries. Some dived head-first and vanished. The lucky ones got rescued by their mates. It was like gold prospectors coming across a particularly rich seam.

Everyone seemed to have their favourite sort of junk. The Skeletons, efficient as ever formed a non-human chain and passed prized ultra-burnable chair legs along the line into the boot of a waiting hearse. Two Mummies bumbled around with a horsehair sofa. They kept bumping into things as they tried to find the exit.

The local chapter of Hell's Gnomes jealously guarded a pile of old motor bike tyres. The Ghouls seemed to go in for old newspapers in a big way and were carting off hundreds of mouldy back issues of *Witch Weekly* and the *Daily Miracle*. Two Were-wolves, having the double advantages of super-human strength and nasty sets of gnashers, got more than their fair share of the ever-popular broken wardrobes. A small Dragon by the name of Arthur made off triumphantly with a whole grand piano, giggling to himself.

A demented-looking furry Thing with a tee shirt which said *Moonmad* raced around madly with an old pram. It was clearly an indecisive sort of Thing, as it kept changing its mind, emptying everything out, and starting all over again. The abandoned junk was then swooped on and picked over by Banshees with carrier bags and a Troll with a stolen super-market trolly.

It was a shocking sight.
So much greed. So much stealing.
And all the brain-child of
one lampless Genie.

"Come in, you two mummies, your time is up," Ali Pali announced through the megaphone, adding "Okay, you can go in now," to a waiting she-demon with a small hand cart. Not surprisingly he was feeling very pleased with himself. Things were looking up. All his carefully laid plans were bearing fruit. Why shortly he'd have enough for that nice little solid silver number he'd always had his eye on. The one with the twirly handle and that elegant spout. The one he'd always fancied. By the end of the night, he'd have enough to buy it outright. If his luck held.

"What's goin' on 'ere then? What you doin' wiv the rubbish?" enquired a passing Zombie from another wood, squinting curiously into the tent. (Zombies are almost as dense as Goblins.)

"I'm cleaning up," explained Ali Pali, and laughed until he choked.

CHAPTER THIRTEEN

TREACHERY

Can you imagine this scene from the air? All the lights and noise and bustle? And can you imagine the effect such a spectacle might have on a posse of twelve well meaning AWOL Broomsticks who have come sick-visiting?

On the whole, the Brooms had had a smooth flight. A bit of minor turbulence here and there, and a small detour to buy Lucozade and grapes but otherwise uneventful. Until they got a bit closer to their destination, that is, and suddenly become aware of *a mysterious glow in the sky*! It appeared to be coming from Pongwiffy's rubbish dump up ahead. Instant panic.

Huh? Glow in the sky? Where? How? Why? What?

Understandably, the Broomsticks were feeling a bit jittery. Bear in mind that they are a law-abiding sort who don't even break the speed limit often, let alone go sneaking off on wild mercy errands without permission. The long, cold flight had done wonders to dampen their enthusiasm. They were already wishing they hadn't come. Already anxious to get back before someone spotted they were missing. Quite honestly, a mysterious glow was something they could have done without. However, having

come this far, the Brooms felt duty bound to investi-
gate. Slowly, hesitantly, keeping close together, they
approached the Dump and peered down.

Nothing could have prepared them for the shock.
They were instantly thrown into confusion. What a
revelation! What a bolt from the blue! They came to a
ragged halt, skittered about a bit, then bobbed
unsteadily in mid-air, skulking behind the odd
whispy bit of cloud and trying to blend in with the
treetops. Eyes on stalks, they stifled screams and
goggled disbelievingly at the scene below. As if to
rub salt into the wound, a sudden puff of wind
tugged one of Ali Pali's posters from a tree trunk and
hurled it skywards. It got all tangled up with
Stumpy's bristles. Stumpy didn't need to read it in
order to twig what was going on.

The Dump had been invaded!

The ultimate crime.

Oooer.

Yes indeed, Pongwiffy's pride and joy was crawling with unsavoury riffraff who, can you believe it,
appeared to be helping themselves. Oh, the bold bla-
tancy of it! Lights, music, theft on a grand scale! Oh,
the deceit of it! The sheer cheek of it! Whatever
would Pongwiffy say?

The Brooms were terribly shocked. Not one of
them had a clue what to do. Uncertainly they milled
about, agitatedly scanning the ground below for any
sign of Woody. It was hopeless. The garden shed
appeared to have been taken over by a fortune-

telling gnome and Woody was nowhere to be seen. Their poor, suffering friend had most probably been carted off by some crazed rubbish-happy lout as part of his/her/its haul. Oh no. Grapes and Get Well cards suddenly seemed inappropriate.

Far below, one of the Hell's Fiends glanced up. Suddenly, hanging about seemed inappropriate as well.

"FLY FOR IT!"

As one, the Brooms turned, pointed towards Crag Hill and took off at a hundred miles per hour, screaming their bristles off. And that's why Pongwiffy, Hugo and Woody, flying along at a sedate five mph, suddenly heard a faint whistling sound. Then, to their great dismay, they were faced with the unsettling sight of twelve stampeding Broomsticks heading straight towards them at incredible speed with no obvious intention of stopping.

"It's the Brooms! They've escaped from the Goblins! They're bolting! Emergency dive!" shrieked Pongwiffy, clutching onto her hat. And Woody did. Only just in time.

With a blast of wind, the Broomsticks passed overhead, missing them by a whisker.

*   *   *   *   *

"Phew! Vell done, Broom. Zat vas a near vun!" remarked Hugo a short while later. At the time, the three of them were clinging precariously to the sharp top of a pine tree.

Woody said nothing. It was still recovering from the shock. After all it had been through, being forced so rudely out of the sky by its own mates was the very last straw.

For once, Pongwiffy had nothing to say either. Mainly because she had a small branch in her mouth, but also because she was so very depressed. Everything seemed to be going wrong. Oh, why oh why did all this have to happen when she should be putting her mind to fund-raising for the Hallowe'en party? It just wasn't fair.

"Come on, Mistress, cheer up," coaxed Hugo, "Look on ze bright side. We find ze Brooms, jah? So! Ze main problem is solved. Und ve still in vun piece. Und I 'ave plan."

"You do?" said Pongwiffy, perking up. "What is it?"

"Ve go 'ome," said Hugo. "Ve climb down zis tree, valk to ze 'ovel und ave a nice cuppa bogwater. Ve cannot be far from 'ome. I pretty sure it over zere, look. Near zat glow in sky."

He waved his paw in a vague southerly direction. Both Pongwiffy and Woody brightened up.

"Agreed," said Pongwiffy. "Tonight's been one long disaster from beginning to end. A nice hot cuppa will do us all the world of good. You go down first, Hugo. Then if I fall, at least one of my feet will have something soft to land on."

"Okay. I go now – but vait! Vat zat?"

"What's what? By the way, I've been thinking. *What glow in the sky?*"

"Sssssh!" hissed Hugo. "Look!"

Silently, he pointed below. Pongwiffy looked down – and nearly fell off her branch in shock. Passing below the very tree in which they perched, shuffled two Mummies. Moonlight glinted off their bandages. Everyone knew them, because they were the only Mummies for a thousand miles. As thieves, they were at a very distinct disadvantage.

"Ees Xotindis and Xstufitu," breathed Hugo. "And, Mistress, look! Look vat zey carry!"

Between them, Xotindis and Xstufitu carried a sofa. But not just any sofa. Oh no. This sofa, until very recently, had enjoyed pride of place in Pongwiffy's own living room! It was the nastiest sofa that anyone could ever dream up in their wildest nightmares. It was exceptionally awful when new, but you should have seen it after Pongwiffy had had it for a few years. It was stained with sloppings and crisp with crumbs. Three springs burst out of the seat. It was old and disgusting, and Pongwiffy loved it.

"AHHHHHHHHHHHHHH! MY SOFA! MINE! STOP THIEF!"

Flustered night birds rose flapping from the trees as the outraged squawk echoed through the woods.

The Mummies instantly recognised who it was, and broke into a panicky run. They did quite well. It's no easy thing to run through a wood with a stolen sofa if you're swathed in bandages and completely blind. They managed at least three steps before Xotindis (the one at the back) caught his toe in a root. Both fell down with a crash and began to unravel.

"Are you all right, Otto?" asked Xstufitu in a muffled voice.

"Not sure yet. What about you, Stufi?" came the reply.

"I think I'm okay. Come on, let's crawl for it!"

"Not so fast, you!"

Pongwiffy placed her foot firmly on the end of Xstufitu's bandage. "Move an inch, and you're unwound!"

"It's a fair cop," said Xstufitu, sitting up and rubbing his elbow. "Get your foot off my bandage, Pongwiffy. It isn't funny to mess with a Mummy's bandages."

"It's not a fair cop, Stufi," objected Xotindis. "We paid good money to get this sofa. It's ours now, Pongwiffy."

"Do you hear that?" remarked Pongwiffy to Hugo and Woody. "Can you believe a walking strip of old rag could tell such shocking lies?"

"Watch it," snapped Xotindis. "We were Pharaohs once, you know. You should mind how you address royalty, Pongwiffy."

"I don't know about addressing royalty," said Pongwiffy grimly. "But I know how to *undress* royalty. I'm going to sit on MY sofa and listen while you two talk. You've got two minutes to tell me exactly what's been going on behind my back. Otherwise, consider yourself unravelled."

Xotindis and Xstufitu looked at each other, and shrugged.

"Weellll," began Xotindis slowly. "There's this Genie. . ."

CHAPTER FOURTEEN

THE REUNION

"Talk about a muck up," said Stinkwart, shaking his head. "One of our worst flops, that."

"I fink I've lost my hat," said Lardo. He had been vainly searching his head for the last five minutes, and was pretty sure that the hat wasn't there. But the rest of the Goblins weren't especially interested.

They were huddled in the bushes bordering the empty Broom park, eating humbugs and arguing about what had gone wrong. The quarrel had started immediately after the botched raid, and was still continuing. (Goblin rows can ramble on for ever, because Goblins repeat themselves so much.)

"I still say it wuz all Plugugly's fault," said Slopbucket meanly, for the hundredth time.

" 'Ere, 'ere," agreed Stinkwart, Hog, Slopbucket, Eyesore and Sproggit, also for the hundredth time.

"The fing is, wuz I wearin' it when I come out tonight?" pondered Lardo.

"Plugugly's a failure," observed Eyesore. "You're a failure, Plugugly."

"I said I wuz sorry," mumbled Plugugly sulkily. He was slumped dejectedly under a blackberry bush, gnawing at his thumbnail in a crestfallen manner. "It were the stress."

"We shoulda chopped it up," insisted young Sproggit. "Chopped it up, like I said in the first place. Shouldn't we, Lardo?"

But Lardo was still concerned about his hat. He had a horrible feeling it had fallen off in the Broom park and was even now lying there in the moonlight for anyone to see. (It was. One of the essential parts of any failed undercover Goblin mission is the leaving of at least one whacking great clue.)

"I'm fed up wiv sittin' 'ere," said Slopbucket suddenly. "I'm cold. I wanna go 'ome."

"I'm cold too. No hat, see," remarked Lardo, pointing to his lumpy bare head. Everyone ignored him. So Lardo snatched Sproggit's hat and put it on his own head. Sproggit, of course, objected, and a brief fight followed. Everyone joined in out of habit, but nobody's heart was really in it.

Hog broke up the fight by passing round the humbugs, and for a short time the Goblins sat in silence, blowing hot, humbuggy breath on their cold fingers and trying not to think about the long walk home.

That was when Macabre (following a hunch) arrived at the Broom park for the first time. She was so shocked to find it deserted that she didn't notice the Goblins in the bushes. She did notice Lardo's hat, though. She swooped down on it with a cry of triumph and bore it away at full gallop.

"What were that?" asked Hog. "I fort I 'eard a noise. Sounded like gallopin' hooves."

"Probably a squirrel," said Eyesore knowledgeably. " 'Ave a look, Sproggit."

Sproggit crawled off into the bushes. He lost his way and was gone quite a long time. When he finally crawled back, the rest of the Goblins had dozed off. Sproggit shrugged, then joined them.

When Macabre returned to the Broom park to hunt for clues more thoroughly, she wondered how she missed them the first time. There they were, only a few yards from the scene of the crime, all snoring like mad, and reeking of peppermint. Scattered all around them was the evidence of a full scale broom-napping attempt. Of the Brooms there was still no sign.

Macabre hugged herself with excitement. She dismounted from Rory and tiptoed over to the sleeping Goblins. Then:

"Wakey wakey!" screeched Macabre, and treated them to a deafening blast on her bagpipes. At the same time Rory let fire with a malicious moo. The Goblins stirred, sat up and blearily knuckled their eyes.

"Stand and deliver! Surrender! Hands oop!"

Macabre had a bossy sort of nature, and loved arresting people. In fact, she always carried a pair of handcuffs in her sporran, in case she ever got the chance to use them. Delightedly, she clapped them on Plugugly then tied up the rest of the Goblins with rope whilst they were still half asleep. She then frogmarched them away from the Broom park, down the hill and into the enemy camp.

"Now look what ah got! Goblins!" bellowed Macabre importantly. "Caught napping at the scene o' the crime, they were. Skulking in yon bushes. Aye. Broomnappers. Every last one."

Seven sleepy, surly Goblins were rudely thrust forward. The assembled Witches gave them the usual charming Witch welcome: they pulled rude faces, jeered, and pelted the captives with bread rolls. Ratsnappy stuck her foot out to trip up Lardo and Bendyshanks poked Eyesore in the leg with a stick. Sludgegooey dabbled her fingers in her mug of tepid bogwater and flicked some in Plugugly's eye. Sproggit got jostled. Stinkwart got hit in the ear with a piece of ham. The Witches were having a wonderful time. What a night it had been. First, the business of Pongwiffy's Broom. That was closely followed by the excitement of the Broomnapping. Then there was the discovery that their Magic wasn't working properly and the State Of Emergency and everything. Now, just when things were beginning to get dull, hey presto! The Broomnappers themselves turn up! The sandwiches were getting low, but the Witches' spirits were running high.

"Boo!"

"Go home, Plugugly!"

"Stand up straight, Slopbucket, you'll trip over your knuckles!"

"What you lot done with our Brooms then, maggot face?"

"Let me through! Let me at 'em! I'm Grandwitch, I get to ask the questions!" shouted Sourmuddle, pushing her way through the crowd to where the Goblins stood in a truculent huddle. Macabre stood to attention and saluted proudly as the boss hobbled up.

"Well done, Macabre. Glad to see somebody's got their wits about them. Right, you Goblins. What have you got to say for yourselves? Caught red-handed, eh?" Sourmuddle cackled, wiggling her fingers in front of their noses in traditional Witch fashion.

"We din do nuffin'," chanted the Goblins automatically.

"Don't be ridiculous. Of course you did."

"Indubitably!" agreed Greymatter. "Place them in detention! Incarcerate them!"

"Make 'em walk the plank!" (Dead Eye Dudley, ex-pirate cat.)

"Guilty! Guilty!" (Everybody else.)

"We din do nuffin'!" chorused the Goblins again. It was what they always said when they were caught redhanded. It was a response guaranteed to

irritate, particularly when they kept saying it. A lot
of hissing and growling and gnashing of teeth and so
on came from the crowd. Barry the vulture flapped
up to a tree, hunched his shoulders and adopted
what he liked to think of as his Threatening Pose.
Snoop the Demon tested his pitchfork for sharpness.
Gaga's bats jostled and squeaked angrily. There was
the ominous sound of claw sharpening.

The Goblins shrugged it off. They'd seen it all
before.

"Oh, come now," hissed Sourmuddle, enjoying
herself. "Of course you've got our Brooms. You've
hidden them somewhere. You're at our mercy, you
might as well tell us where they are. Come along,
come along."

"We ain't got yer stoopid Brooms," muttered
Sproggit. "If you must know, they flewed off on
their own. We din do nuffin'."

"Oooh, what a fibber!"

"Just fly off, did he say? Our Brooms? A likely
story!"

"Turn 'im into a frog, Sourmuddle, make an
example of 'im!"

Sproggit shrugged and looked like he didn't care
much – which indeed he didn't. Frog spells always
wore off in time. Sooner or later he'd end up a Goblin
again, so who cared? What were a few days of forced
swimming and mayflies for breakfast in the great
scheme of things? But it didn't come to that anyway,
because:

"Hold it, girls! Do you see what I see?" said Bendyshanks suddenly, through a mouthful of Witches' Pride and wartleberry jam. And she pointed upwards. Everyone — Witches, Familiars and Goblins — turned their attention on the sky. All mouths dropped open.

The sky was full of Brooms! They whizzed about overhead, obviously preparing for touch down.

"They're back!" went up the surprised cry. "Our Brooms are back!"

"That's funny," said Sourmuddle. "I wonder where they've been? Looks like you Goblins didn't have 'em after all. You arrested 'em for nothing, Macabre. What a pity, eh?"

Macabre was lying full length on the ground pummelling it with her fists, and didn't reply.

"Told you," chorused the Goblins. "We din do nuffin'. Told you." And Plugugly added, "Dey runned away, like Sproggit said. So yah boo sucks to you, Macabre."

Just at that moment, Sharkadder came hurrying up. After spending virtually the whole of this book on bad terms with Pongwiffy, she was finally beginning to come round. It was the look on Pongwiffy's face when she flew off all on her own. All hurt and forlorn. Sharkadder had almost called her back and said she'd go with her, but she'd had an egg roll in her mouth at the time and couldn't. Now she felt bad. Pongwiffy was awful, but best friends were best friends.

"Where's Pong?" asked Sharkadder, scanning the sky. "Why isn't she with them?"

"Who knows?" said Sourmuddle, unconcerned. "Who cares? I tell you what, there's something funny about those Brooms."

She was right. Just at that moment, the Brooms touched down. It wasn't a neat, orderly touch-down. As touch-downs go, it was a mess. There was a hasty, hysterical quality about it. There was a lot of flurried skidding and bumping and misjudgement. And you only had to look at the Brooms' stricken expressions to know that they were upset about something. They jiggled up and down and pointed urgently to the sky.

"Oh dear," groaned Sourmuddle. "Not again. It's like an 'orrible recurring nightmare. They're trying to warn us about something. I don't suppose anyone . .?"

No. No one was prepared to speak Wood.

"Not even for the sake of National Security?" coaxed Sourmuddle.

Not even for that. As one, the Witches folded their arms, tapped their feet and suddenly became fascinated by their own dirty fingernails.

Meanwhile, the Brooms ran around in small circles, wringing their hands helplessly and getting in a terrible tizzy.

"Well, someone's got to find out what they're on about, and it won't be me," insisted Sourmuddle. "Because I'm boss. Come along. A volunteer to speak

Wood. I'm not sitting through charades again."

"I'll do it," said Sharkadder, suddenly stepping forward. "I'll do it for the sake of Pongwiffy, because despite everything, she's my best friend."

Dead Eye Dudley spat disgustedly.

"Well, I'm sorry Duddles, but she is," insisted Sharkadder. "And I'm sure you wouldn't *really* want anything awful to happen to Hugo."

"Yes I would," said Dudley.

"We've all forgotten something," remarked Greymatter. "Our Magic's still not working. I don't suppose you can even remember the spell, Sharkadder. Can anyone remember that language spell? The one with the side effects? I'm sure I can't."

Greymatter was right. No one could. Mind you, no one tried very hard.

"Oh, what a pity," said Sharkadder, trying not to sound too relieved. "That's that, then."

"No more charades!" repeated Sourmuddle firmly. "Too boring. Takes too long. Look, I've had enough excitement for one night. Personally, I'm for cancelling the State of Emergency and going home. Whatever the important message is, it can probably wait until tomorrow. . ."

"Wait! Look what I've found! This explains everything!"

Sludgegooey was urgently waving the poster which she had just discovered entangled with Stumpy's bristles. Very sensibly, Stumpy had hung on to it. In fact, Stumpy had been trying to draw her attention to it for some time, but Sludgegooey was a bit slow on the uptake.

"Listen!" said Sludgegooey. And read it out.

There was an instant's shocked silence, then a howl of rage went up! To think of it! The Brooms, limp with relief, sagged against trees and fanned themselves. It took a while for the Goblins' slow brains to grasp the significance of the words on the poster – but when they did, they started kicking themselves for missing the sale of the century. Just think. All that effort wasted on a failed Broomnapping when they could have strolled along to the Dump and helped themselves to as much rubbish as they could carry for a fiver.

"So that's it!" said Sourmuddle. "Genie Enterprises, eh? I should have guessed. Only a Genie would have the cheek. In the words of my old mother, never trust a flashy dresser, especially if he lives in a lamp. Mind you, I'm surprised a Genie would have the skill to dismantle that Wall of Pongwiffy's. I've never put much store by that gawdy oriental Magic myself. Oh well. You live and learn."

At long last, all was clear. Except that nobody was very sure how the Goblins fitted in. Or why the Brooms had gone off all by themselves. Or where Pongwiffy was. Or who was the mastermind behind Genie Enterprises, and how was he able to work such an elaborate fiddle unless he'd had inside help? Come to think of it, all wasn't clear by a long way.

"Well, one thing's certain," continued Sourmuddle. "This here Genie Enterprises isn't getting away with it. We'll go and sort him out. RIGHT NOW."

"Whoopee!" bellowed Macabre, brightening up. Eagerly, she began stuffing stale bread rolls into her sporran for ammunition.

"Witches, to your Broomsticks!" ordered Sourmuddle. "Last one on's a goody goody!"

The Witches didn't need telling twice (except for Bonidle, who had to be told several times). They vaulted onto their Broomsticks. There was a drone of bagpipes, dischordant wails on violins, and the

sound of knuckles
cracking. Then,
with a good selection
of wild cackling cries,
they rose
into
the sky.

"Tallyho!" shrieked
Sourmuddle as her
Broomstick plunged and
reared, as over-excited
as a highly-strung race horse.
"Follow me, girls! To the Dump!"

"To the dump, to the dump, to the dump, dump, dump!" sang everybody, and seconds later, they were gone. Plugugly, Stinkwart, Hog, Slopbucket, Lardo, Eyesore and Sproggit were left behind, still tied up but not so tight that they couldn't shuffle over and eat the remains of the sandwiches.

CHAPTER FIFTEEN

THE BATTLE FOR THE DUMP

The Battle For The Dump has, of course, passed into Witch folklore. That's because the Witches won. (Battles which the Witches lose tend not to pass into folklore. They pass into oblivion.) The Battle For The Dump, being a victory, got talked about and mulled over and relived for months afterwards. Tactics were discussed. Personal acts of heroism and bravery were trotted out again and again by Witches, Familiars and Brooms alike. Everyone claimed a stunning – no, let's be honest, *unbelievable* - personal success rate. To hear everyone talk, you'd have thought that she, he or it had won the entire battle alone and unaided.

The Battle For The Dump began as Ali Pali was on the point of lighting up his fourth cigar. He was also on his second cash register, having worn out the first by ringing up so many five pound notes. What a night it had been! His carpet bag was bursting at the seams. Most of the choice pieces of rubbish had been snapped up long ago - yet still the punters came. Just as Ali Pali would think the crowds were thinning a little, and wonder whether he ought to think of packing up and clearing out, more eager junk hunters would arrive waving fistfuls of fivers, desperate to wade in amongst it all.

A whole crowd of Vampires (bonfire fangatics

all) were bussed in. So rife was the spirit of competition, some of the keener types went home to get another fiver and *had more than the one go!* The tea hut was doing a roaring trade, and the badge seller had run out. A steady stream of rubbish poured out of the Dump, which by now was beginning to look sadly depleted.

"Rubbish Fever," thought Ali Pali with a superior little chuckle. "That's what they've got. Junk on the brain. Bonfire crazy, the poor saps."

(Genies don't go in for Hallowe'en much. They feel they're much too sophisticated to jump around bonfires on chilly hills. If they celebrate it at all, it's likely to be lying on some silken couch eating grapes, or an intimate little supper party in some friend's lamp.)

Ali Pali certainly had cause for celebration. Everything had gone so smoothly. Dismantling the Wall of Smell had been simple, because Pongwiffy had given him the recipe (and once you have the recipe, you can easily work out the antidote). Jamming the Witches' magic signals just in case they tried to "ring home" as it were, had been a masterstroke. The spell had come straight out of one of Pongwiffy's own spell books. And as for the transformation of the Dump - well, it was beyond question the best thing he had ever done.

"Rich!" crowed Ali to himself. "Rich beyond my wildest dreams! I think I'll skip the lamp and go straight for the palace!"

His smug little chuckle turned into a great, triumphant cackle. No more of that Your Wish Is My Command stuff. He could retire. Why, if he wanted, he could afford his *own* Genie! Then, as is often the way, something happened to spoil it all.

"Excuse me, Mr Pali," said a voice. It was the Thing in the Moonmad tee shirt. "I think you got company," it said. And pointed up. Ali Pali looked and gave a little whistle. The night sky was suddenly

full of screaming Witches. Even as he looked, they banked steeply, grouped into battle formation and prepared to attack.

"Oh-oh. Closing time, I think," said Ali Pali, snapping his fingers at his carpet bag, which immediately yawned open. Quickly and efficiently, he began to pack.

As he did so, the screaming Witches swooped down upon the Dump like angry hornets, buzzing the unsuspecting punters and making them scatter in all directions. Some dropped to the ground and hid their heads. Others took to their heels and ran into the trees for cover, getting away with whatever they could. A few put up a token resistance, but the Witches had the advantage of surprise, so there wasn't much point. By far the most sensible course was to drop the loot and scarper. Fast.

Quite a few made it to safety. The Hell's Gnomes had their bikes, and made a clean getaway. So did the Trolls, the Yeti, the fortune-telling gnome and the Thing with the Moonmad tee shirt. The Skeletons regretfully abandoned Pongwiffy's last kitchen chair, piled into their hearse and drove off with an impressive screaming of brakes. Once out of the danger zone, they broke open a bottle of champagne: I say, what a laugh eh? Pass the corkscrew, Nigel!

Others weren't so lucky. The Ghouls were terribly slow movers. Every time they struggled to their knees they'd get buzzed again, and would slowly topple head first into the Dump to yet another mouthful of something awful. And they weren't the only unlucky ones. When it came to ham roll throwing, Macabre was mustard. Many a raider of the Lost Dump staggered home with hot ears and black eyes that night. Others got pinched, scratched or had their hair pulled. One of the Werewolves got flapped at most unpleasantly by a bunch of Bats. The greediest Troll received a nasty peck from Barry. A She-Demon got clonked by a Broomstick and needed a plaster.

Safe in his stripey tent, Ali Pali scooped up the last of the loot. His plan was to vanish instantly and as discreetly as possible (no green smoke and no bang). He would make for some quiet, oriental haven and go underground for a bit, until the heat died off. Then, as soon as everyone had forgotten or ceased to care, he and his carpet bag would emerge, head for the nearest estate agent and spend, spend, spend!

That was the plan, anyway. And it might have worked, too, if only he had been just that little bit quicker. He had just snapped the bulging carpet bag shut, and was looking round the tent to make sure he hadn't forgotten anything, when he heard a noise behind him. He whirled round and came face to face with . . .

Pongwiffy! Behind her, twiggy arms folded menacingly, stood her Broom, and on her shoulder perched the most ferocious-looking Hamster Ali had ever seen in his life.

Ali Pali noticed several things. He noticed that Pongwiffy was holding an extremely perky-looking Wand. In her other hand she held a small, green, ominous bottle. He also noticed uncomfortably that she was smiling.

"Hello, Ali," purred Pongwiffy. "Going somewhere?"

*

Much, much later, after all the fun was over and everyone had gone home, a gaggle of Goblins trailed through Witchway Wood. They were pushing a squeaking cart full of ropes, pitchforks, nets, and so on. They looked just about all in. It had taken them ages to bite through Macabre's knots and free themselves. Then they'd had to drag back up to the Broom park to pick up all their equipment. Then they'd set off on the long walk home.

What a scene of carnage greeted them as they squeaked along under the trees. Wonderingly, they stared around. At the crashed wardrobe. At the abandoned mangle. At the dropped newspapers. At that thoroughly awful sofa. Everywhere there were pieces of garbage and scattered bread rolls. All pointing to a hasty flight.

"Must 'ave bin some punch-up," said Slopbucket, awed.

"Yer," agreed Sproggit, rubbing his eyes blearily. "An' we missed it."

"I wonder who won?" yawned Lardo.

"The Witches, of course," said Hog. "They always do. I wonder why that is?"

"Well, one fing's fer sure," said Eyesore with a sneer. "They won't be the only ones wiv a good bonfire this year. Looks like the uvvers got away wiv a pile o' stuff. Yerp, there'll be some good blazes this Hallowe'en."

" 'Cept fer ours, o' course," put in Stinkwart. "It's all your fault, Plugugly."

But something was the matter with Plugugly. His eyes were rolling wildly and his face had gone very red. Funny, strangled noises were coming from his mouth. Finally, he spoke.

"I fink — wait, it's comin' — lads, I fink I gorra 'nother idear!"

There was alarmed consternation from the other Goblins. Cries of "Oh no, anyfing but that!"

"No, reelly, wait a tick, I 'ave, I reelly 'ave. An' it's simple. Listen, we got the cart, aint we? An' dere's no one about. An' dere's all dis rubbish lying around, right? Now den. *What's ter stop us pickin' it up an' takin' it 'ome?*"

He was right. There was nothing to stop them. It was a brilliant plan, and exactly what they did. They also collected up the bread rolls. So, fans of the Goblins will be delighted to know that at least something turned out right for them that night.

CHAPTER SIXTEEN

FRIENDS AGAIN

One week later. The sun rose early on the morning of Hallowe'en — but not as early as Witch Sharkadder. When day dawned crisp and clear, she had already been hard at work for a good hour. She was seated before her mirror in a pink dressing gown, Getting Ready. Her head bristled with hedgehog hair rollers, and she was waiting for her mud pack to dry. Now and then, she took careful, dainty sips from a bowl of mouseli. The party was that very night, and she did like to take her time on these special occasions. Only nineteen hours to go, when all was said and done.

She was enjoying herself tremendously, because she had a whole new range of sinister little pots to play with. Pongwiffy had bought them for her, like the good friend she was. (What Sharkadder didn't know was that Pongwiffy had paid for them with her Magic Coin, the one which always ends up back in her own purse. In fact, there was going to be quite a bit of trouble about the new range of make-up — but that's another story.)

Sharkadder was determined to do a particularly magnificent job. It was essential that she should get the make-up just right for the fancy dress parade. In her dual role as judge and participant, she owed it to the rest of them to show how it should be done.

Getting the new make-up and being reinstated as judge had all been part of making friends with Pongwiffy again. They have been best friends now for a record time. Seven days. Ever since the Night Of The Battle, as it came to be called. (Although Sharkadder thought of it more as The Night Of Our Last Row. And the Coal Shovel and Rake referred to it as The Night We Got Slung Out Of Our Own Shed. And Woody thought of it as The Night Of My Great Shame. And Plugugly thought of it as De Night I 'Ad All Dem Idears. And Bendyshank's snake, Seething Steve, thought of it as The Night I Learned To Do A Reef Knot. It just depended on your point of view, really.)

Anyway. If the truth be known, Sharkadder felt rather badly about that night. Yes, Pongwiffy had behaved stupidly, but that was nothing new. She, Sharkadder, hadn't really helped matters. She had been generally unforgiving and not at all helpful to a friend in need. Poor old Pong. Everything had gone wrong for her. All right, so it all worked out in the end, and they had come out of the whole thing with oodles of money, but it had been a terrible price to pay. Pongwiffy's view from her hovel window had changed. The Dump, once a vision of mouldering loveliness, was a shadow of its former self. Pongwiffy was deeply attached to her rubbish, and it would take her a long time to get over such a great loss. Luckily, arrangements for the party had taken her mind off things.

"Dear old Pong," thought Sharkadder, coming over all sentimental. She looked fondly over at the magnificent costume, hired at considerable expense, now hanging in splendour from a hook. Sharkadder hadn't hesitated in choosing what she was going as. She was going as the Wicked Queen in Snow White. It was a lifetime's ambition. She couldn't wait to put it all on, especially the dress. As she thought of wearing That Dress, she almost allowed an excited grin to crack her face - but that would never do. The mud pack didn't really allow for smiling. Time for the nails now. They had to be filed to points and painted blood red. As soon as they were dry, oh goody goody, she could put the dress on! She picked up the file, and carefully, oh so carefully, began to rub. Then:

"Yoo hoo! Sharky! It's me, Pongwiffy. Can I come in?"

Sharkadder leapt six inches in the air and two tragic things happened. Her mud pack cracked and she broke a nail.

"Morning," said Pongwiffy, bustling in, making for the kettle. "I can't stay, I'm far too busy. I just popped by to wish my very best friend a Happy Hallowe'en. I meant to buy you a present, but you know how it is. Oooh! Mouseli. My favourite cereal."

Sharkadder got herself under control with difficulty. She bit her lip and reached for the glue, reminding herself of the seven-day friendship record.

"All right, Pong, you've said hello," she said. "Now go. I don't want you hanging round here all morning. Not when I'm Getting Ready."

"I'm ready already," said Pongwiffy, who looked exactly the same as usual. "I'm absolutely ready. I'm the Witch from Hansel and Gretel. The one with the house of sweets."

"But you look exactly the same as always," said Sharkadder.

"No I don't," said Pongwiffy. "If you look carefully, you'll notice several boiled sweets stuck around the hem of my skirt. There were more, but I keep eating them."

Sharkadder shrugged. It didn't really matter what anyone else wore, as long as she was the Wicked Queen. In That Dress. "How's your Broom?" she asked, just to be polite.

"Much better thanks. I left it outside with yours.

With strict instructions not to go flying off on its own again, ha ha.''

(Indeed, Woody was slowly recovering with the aid of its fellow Brooms, who had formed a support group. The general feeling seemed to be that, whilst it didn't exactly deserve an award for distinguished service, it didn't need its nose rubbed in it either. Woody fans will be pleased to know that within a couple of weeks, it stopped jumping at every noise, and within a month it had forgotten the entire incident. So had the rest of them. Brooms have long, thin brains that don't leave much room for memory.)

"And how are the party arrangements going?" asked Sharkadder as she attempted to fix her ruined nail.

"Oh, fine, fine. Everything's under control. We start off with the fancy dress parade on the dot of midnight. I've booked the Witchway Rhythm Boys and they'll play marching music while we all walk round in our costumes. Pierre de Gingerbeard's doing the cake. He's expensive, but money's no object this year."

"Good old Pierre," nodded Sharkadder. "He's my cousin, you know."

"I know. Oh, and I've hired a couple of Yetis to run the barbecue. Macabre's in charge of the games. Ratsnappy's bringing the funny hats. Gaga's crackers, as usual. I've got Scrofula putting the chocolate spiders into the party bags. The entertainment's all organised. Agglebag and Bagaggle will do a violin recital, I'm afraid, and Macabre's insisting on playing her bagpipes, but Sludgegooey's promised to try to hide them. I've cut Greymatter's poetry reading down to thirty seconds. I've booked a conjuror and a tap-dancing dwarf and a singing leprechaun. Oh, and some gnome who tells fortunes. It's going to be the best party in Witch History."

"Sounds lovely," said Sharkadder." I can't wait."

"The only thing that won't be up to scratch is the bonfire," said Pongwiffy with a sigh. "To be frank, I'm ashamed of it. But we all know who to thank for *that*, don't we?"

"We certainly do," agreed Sharkadder. "I was going to ask you about him. What did you do with him? In the finish?"

"What do you think? I bottled him," said Pongwiffy grimly. "He works for me now."

"Oh, what a good idea," said Sharkadder, clapping her hands. "Are you finding him useful?"

"Yes and no," said Pongwiffy. And from a pocket in her cardigan, she produced the small, ominous green bottle with an ill-fitting cork stuffed in the top to keep it stoppered. You didn't have to be a Genie to know it would be cramped in there and probably very draughty. Pongwiffy tossed it casually on to the table.

"Go on, spit in it if you like. I do, often. He's not in right now. I've sent him off to Crag Hill to redo the party decorations. That'll teach him to interfere with

Walls Of Smell that I build. Hugo's gone to keep an eye on him.''

''Why?'' asked Sharkadder. ''You think he'll try to escape?''

''Oh no. It's just to make sure he gets the decorations right. He's good at transformations, I'll grant you that, but everything he does always has that tinselly sort of look. I keep telling him. Gloomier, I say. Easy on the fairy lights. Forget the incense. This is a Witch party, and we Witches don't go in for all those cheap special effects.''

''How does he like the accommodation?'' asked Sharkadder with a sneer. ''Not up to his usual standards, I suppose?''

''He does nothing but moan. I'm freeing him after the party. It's all very well having a slave to do all the work, but every time he appears he's got a list of complaints as long as your arm. He's threatening me with the Genie's Union now. He reckons I'm only entitled to three wishes by law, then I have to release him.''

They both sighed and shook their heads.

''What a cheek,'' they tutted in chorus.

''What's even worse,'' confided Pongwiffy, lowering her voice. ''What's even *more* worrying, he says he'll spread it around that I – you know - gave him our secret code numbers and told him the recipe for the Wall Of Smell.''

''Well, of course, he's right,'' Sharkadder was quick to point out. ''It was all your own fault, Pong.''

"I know, I know," said Pongwiffy uncomfortably. "I thought we weren't going to talk about that. You promised you wouldn't tell."

"Of course I won't," said Sharkadder stoutly. "I'm your best friend, remember?"

"Still," said Pongwiffy, brightening up. "Things could have been worse. At least I caught him before he made off with the money. And you and I are friends again. And the Broom's better. And none of us had to speak Wood. And tonight we're going to have the best Hallowe'en party in the history of the universe!"

"And I'm going to be the Wicked Queen," added Sharkadder.

"So you are, so you are. And with that costume and your looks, I'm sure you'll have no hesitation in awarding yourself first prize in the fancy dress."

"Oh I will," agreed Sharkadder confidently. "Thanks, Pong."

"You're welcome," said Pongwiffy. "Er — any chance of breakfast?"

Meeooooo oscooof

Hugo firmly affixed to Dudley's Tail

ZZZZ

ZZZZ

POST SCRIPT

For those of you who like to know these things, here are a few details.

The Witches' Party
Highly successful. Unanimously voted Best Hallowe'en Party Yet. Here are the results of the *Fancy Dress Competition*:

1st Prize:
The Wicked Queen from Snow White and her Faithful Cat (Sharkadder and Dudley)

2nd Prize:
Little Bo Peep (Sourmuddle. Snoop declined to be a sheep)

3rd Prize:
Joan of Arc and her Trusty Steed (Macabre and Rory)

Runners up:
Tweedledee and Tweedledum (Ag and Bag)

Highly Commended:
Gaga, for her highly individual interpretation of a storm in a tea cup.

No mention at all of:
Happy the Dwarf (Ratsnappy)
The Good Witch Glinda (Sludgegooey)
The Witches on the Blasted Heath (Greymatter, Bendyshanks and Scrofula)
Sleeping Beauty and Friend (Bonidle and the Sloth)
The Sweet House Witch (Pongwiffy)

Judges:
Sharkadder, Ali Pali (who was uncorked for the evening) and one of the Witchway Rhythm Boys (a small Dragon named Arthur).

Sharkadder, Sourmuddle, Macabre, Agglebag and Bagaggle and Gaga thought the results exceptionally fair. Everyone else disagreed. So, as well as all the other lovely things that were laid on, Pongwiffy's famed Hallowe'en Party included an enjoyable little punch-up towards the end. Everyone agreed that the bonfire wasn't quite up to scratch this year, though.

Other Snippets of Information:
The Goblins had their best ever Hallowe'en. Not only was their bonfire huge, they had all those bread rolls. Plus, the Witches sent over a crate of past-the-sell-by-date blackcurrant brew as a gesture of ill-will. To the Goblins, who live mostly on salt-flavoured water and boiled nettles, it tasted lovely.

Ali Pali took advantage of the fight that broke out after the fancy dress parade, and got away. The last time he was heard of, he was flogging second-hand flying carpets to Zombies, so the likelihood is that by now he is a very rich Genie indeed with a lamp in town and another one in the country.

Pongwiffy and Sharkadder broke friends again during the party. All over something Hugo said to Dudley. But that hardly comes as news, does it?

Greymatter's Poem (*All thirty seconds*)

What an entertaining, scintillating,
awe-inspiring party!
What a merry celebration, what a spree!
What a cause for jubilation
right across our great Witch nation!
What a nasty look Pongwiffy's giving me. . . .

Choosing a brilliant book
can be a tricky business...
but not any more

www.puffin.co.uk

The best selection of books at your fingertips

So get clicking!

Searching the site is easy – you'll find
what you're looking for at the click of a mouse,
from great authors to brilliant books and more!

Everyone's got different taste . . .

I like stories that make me laugh

Animal stories are definitely my favourite

I'd say fantasy is the best

I like a bit of romance

It's got to be adventure for me

I really love poetry

I like a good mystery

Whatever you're into, we've got it covered . . .

www.puffin.co.uk

Psst!
What's happening?

sneakpreviews@puffin

For all the inside information on the hottest new books,

click on the Puffin

www.puffin.co.uk

hotnews@puffin

Hot off the press!
You'll find all the latest exclusive Puffin news here

Where's it happening?
Check out our author tours and events programme

Best-sellers
What's hot and what's not? Find out in our charts

E-mail updates
Sign up to receive all the latest news
straight to your e-mail box

Links to the coolest sites
Get connected to all the best author web sites

Book of the Month
Check out our recommended reads

www.puffin.co.uk

Read more in Puffin

For complete information about books available from Puffin – and Penguin – and how to order them, contact us at the appropriate address below. Please note that for copyright reasons the selection of books varies from country to country.

www.puffin.co.uk

In the United Kingdom: Please write to Dept EP, Penguin Books Ltd, Bath Road, Harmondsworth, West Drayton, Middlesex UB7 0DA

In the United States: Please write to Penguin Putnam Inc., P.O. Box 12289, Dept B, Newark, New Jersey 07101–5289 or call 1–800–788–6262

In Canada: Please write to Penguin Books Canada Ltd, 10 Alcorn Avenue, Suite 300, Toronto, Ontario M4V 3B2

In Australia: Please write to Penguin Books Australia Ltd, P.O. Box 257, Ringwood, Victoria 3134

In New Zealand: Please write to Penguin Books (NZ) Ltd, Private Bag 102902, North Shore Mail Centre, Auckland 10

In India: Please write to Penguin Books India Pvt Ltd, 11 Panscheel Shopping Centre, Panscheel Park, New Delhi 110 017

In the Netherlands: Please write to Penguin Books Netherlands bv, Postbus 3507, NL–1001 AH Amsterdam

In Germany: Please write to Penguin Books Deutschland GmbH, Metzlerstrasse 26, 60594 Frankfurt am Main

In Spain: Please write to Penguin Books S. A., Bravo Murillo 19, 1° B, 28015 Madrid

In Italy: Please write to Penguin Italia s.r.l., Via Felice Casati 20, I–20124 Milano

In France: Please write to Penguin France S. A., 17 rue Lejeune, F–31000 Toulouse

In Japan: Please write to Penguin Books Japan, Ishikiribashi Building, 2–5–4, Suido, Bunkyo-ku, Tokyo 112

In South Africa: Please write to Longman Penguin Southern Africa (Pty) Ltd, Private Bag X08, Bertsham 2013

Choosing a brilliant book
can be a tricky business...
but not any more

www.puffin.co.uk

The best selection of books at your fingertips

So get clicking!

Searching the site is easy – you'll find
what you're looking for at the click of a mouse,
from great authors to brilliant books and more!